ERRAND OF VENGEANCE

KILLING BLOW

STAR TREK®
THE ORIGINAL SERIES

book two

⟨ ERRAND OF VENGEANCE ⟩

KILLING BLOW

Kevin Ryan

**Based upon STAR TREK®
created by Gene Roddenberry**

POCKET BOOKS
NEW YORK   LONDON   TORONTO   SYDNEY   SINGAPORE

An *Original* Publication of POCKET BOOKS

POCKET BOOKS, a division of Simon & Schuster, Inc.
1230 Avenue of the Americas, New York, NY 10020

This book is published by Pocket Books, a division of Simon & Schuster, Inc., under exclusive license from Paramount Pictures.

ISBN: 0-7434-4602-X

First Pocket Books printing August 2002

10 9 8 7 6 5 4 3 2 1

POCKET and colophon are registered trademarks of Simon & Schuster, Inc.

For information regarding special discounts for bulk purchases, please contact Simon & Schuster Special Sales at 1-800-456-6798 or business@simonandschuster.com

Printed in the U.S.A.

For Misha and Kevie

Acknowledgments

Thanks once again to Gene Roddenberry and all the creative people who have brought the Klingons to life. And thanks again to Marc Okrand for his work on the Klingon language and his three books *The Klingon Dictionary, The Klingon Way,* and *Klingon for the Galactic Traveler.* Thanks also to the Klingon Language Institute for more helpful translations.

And thanks to Mike Okuda for his patient technical and general Star Trek advice. Once again, *The Star Trek Encyclopedia* and the *Star Trek Chronology* by Mike Okuda and Denise Okuda were indispensable to me as I worked. This book also owes a debt to the *Star Trek: The Next Generation Technical Manual* by Mike Okuda and Rick Sternbach.

Special thanks to my friend Larry Brantley for his advice on things military and to my friends Anthony Steele and Scott McFadden for their patience.

And finally, thanks to my wife, Paullina, who once again provided many thoughtful comments and suggestions. And thanks to my children Natasha, Misha, Kevie, and Tania for their great patience with Dad.

bItuHlaHbe'chugh blquvlaHbe'

("If you cannot be shamed you cannot be honored.")

—KLINGON PROVERB

Prologue

KLINGON BATTLE CRUISER *D'K TAHG*
KLINGON SPACE

KAREL SLEPT FITFULLY.

When he opened his eyes he was looking at his brother Kell—not as he would have been now, but as he was when they were children. Kell was eight and Karel twelve.

"I'm going with you," Kell said. His voice was full of all the force his eight years could muster. It took an effort for Karel not to laugh.

"It is impossible. You are too young and it is too dangerous," their mother said, appearing at the door.

Karel did not question the fact that he was standing outside his family home on Qo'noS, or that his mother was there, or that his brother Kell was young and still alive.

The logic of dreams told him these things were so and he believed them. By force of will he pushed down the dim beginnings of questions. He was too pleased to see his brother to allow them to remain.

"I am no coward, Mother," Kell said, gripping his *mek'leth* sword firmly.

"No one is saying you are a coward, but only a fool faces a trial before he is ready for it," their mother said.

"Karel was my age when he went on his first hunt," Kell said.

Mother shook her head in exasperation.

It was true, but Karel had been bigger at the same age. He had also simply been more ready. Besides the additional danger because of his smaller size, Kell was more squeamish than Karel had been at the same age. He might falter when immediate action was necessary, and such a mistake on a hunt could be fatal.

"Karel, talk to him," Mother said.

Both his brother and mother looked to him now.

His brother's eyes were full of expectation that seemed to demand he be taken seriously as a Klingon and a warrior. The look should have been laughable on someone Kell's age. But it was not. He might not have had size, strength, or years, but he was determined.

Karel knew that if he said no, his brother would forgive him—but he found that he wanted to do something to nurture a determination so strong.

"You are not ready," Karel said.

"I am—" Kell began.

"You are not!" Karel shouted over the younger Klingon's protests. "But today you have an opportunity to prove me wrong."

Before Mother could voice her own protests, Karel continued, "You must prove it by staying by my side and doing what I say."

Relief visibly washed over Kell's face as he nodded vigorously.

Karel said, "I will look after him, Mother."

Karel could tell she was not happy, but she was satisfied. She was their father's wife and would not let fear rule her.

She looked seriously at Kell and said, "Let your foe know the strength of your blood."

Kell nodded seriously as Karel picked up his own *mek'leth*. They walked in silence down a path to the edge of the woods near the family farm.

The brothers met another four Klingon boys of about Karel's age. They immediately shot glances at Kell, who met the gazes with an iron stare, daring them to challenge his right to participate in the hunt.

None did. The small group had learned to show respect to Kell—Karel had seen to that. Though neither the oldest or biggest Klingon of the group, Karel had established himself as their leader several seasons ago.

The group walked on to the edge of the cultivated fields of Karel and Kell's farm. Once inside the woods, they walked on to the spot where they always began their hunts. As they looked for signs, the group spread out in their familiar pattern, with Kell staying close to his brother.

Mourl was the first to find something and whispered, "Over here."

The others converged on Mourl's find and saw the small piece of fur-covered flesh on the ground.

Karel gave a silent nod to Mourl, who began looking for the trail. Though the smallest of the group—next to Kell—Mourl was the best tracker.

After a short time, Mourl had crept behind a heavily thorned bush and pointed straight ahead. Karel and the others peered over the bush and saw the *targ* lying down and watching over its larger prey in the center of a small clearing.

Quickly testing the air, Karel confirmed that they were downwind of the beast. Pleased, Karel used a hand motion to tell the others to wait.

Wild *targs* were never docile, but they were less aggressive after a large meal. Speed and reactions were slowed. The difference would mean the difference between a successful hunt and an unsuccessful one. For the hunters, it often meant the difference between life and death.

These were *targs,* after all.

A sound of movement sounded behind the *targ,* whose head spun around to look for the disturbance. Karel and the others froze.

The sound had come from the other side of the clearing, but the *targ* would be extra alert now.

Scanning the group, Karl was pleased to see that Kell was frozen in place. The only movement was the small rise and fall of the young Klingon's chest as he breathed.

Kell also had a look of relaxed concentration, one that Karel knew mirrored his own expression. He also knew that Kell was hyperalert and ready to move on an instant's notice. It was one of the *Mok'bara* techniques that Karel himself had taught his brother.

The others had not studied the Klingon martial art and were getting restless, their bodies giving in to small, involuntary movements.

Slowly, Karel raised his head above the thorns in

front of them. The *targ* was sitting there, guarding its prey...but not eating.

It was maddening, and Karel knew that sooner or later one of the young Klingons with him would give away their position and they would be facing a hungry *targ* determined to protect its catch.

Karel knew he had to do something quickly. He motioned for the others to take their positions.

They got up slowly—but not silently, Karel noted with displeasure. However, eight-year-old Kell was stealthier than many older, bigger, and more experienced hunters.

Sparing a look at the *targ,* Karel was pleased to see that it had apparently not heard or paid attention to the noise. *Kahless is forgiving today,* Karel thought.

Strangely, the *targ* had not begun eating yet. Usually, a *targ* would not hunt if it was not hungry. This one had no interest in its food.

Well, Karel and his friends had taken on hungry *targs* before. Yet, he had not wanted to take the additional risk with Kell there.

For now, it could not be helped.

Karel slowly backed away as the others formed a line in front of and on either side of him. They would form a rough pincer with Karel and Kell at the apex.

Karel would make noise to attract the *targ*. When it charged, the others would lash out with their *mek'leths,* weakening it as it charged Karel and his brother. Then Karel would have to strike the final blow, or face the wrath of the charging *targ*.

All Klingon hunts ended with such a confrontation between the two combatants, a confrontation that could have only one victor—and one survivor.

Then the largest and oldest of the group made a mistake that changed the nature of the hunt. The big Klingon stepped on a stick, which snapped under his foot.

Instantly, the *targ* was on its feet and moving. The Klingons were far from being in position and far from ready. Suddenly Karel was certain this hunt would end badly.

Then Karel heard the squealing of *targ* young and knew with complete certainty that *badly* would not begin to describe this hunt by the time it was done. He spared his brother a glance—Kell's face showed alertness but not panic.

"A nest?" Kell whispered.

Karel nodded. They had stumbled on a *targ* who was not just protecting a fresh kill but a litter of young, who were hidden in the nearby bush.

When the *targ* was lying next to its prey, it was collecting information about the Klingon hunting party and assessing the threat to its young. In effect, it was planning its own hunt.

Targs were not particularly intelligent, but they were efficient hunters and fierce protectors of their offspring.

And this one was very, very angry.

Since the Klingons were just a few meters away from the bush and not even close to their hunting positions, the *targ* charged the nearest target, Mourl, who had turned to run.

It was a bad mistake. Facing an uninjured charging *targ* with a *mek'leth* was difficult if a Klingon met the attack head-on. If a *targ* caught an unlucky Klingon from behind...

Karel quickly saw what Mourl was trying to do as the

Klingon headed for a nearby tree. It was not a dignified way for a warrior to survive an encounter with a *targ,* but survival, not dignity, was clearly Mourl's primary concern.

Still, Karel saw immediately that it would not work.

"Mourl," Karel shouted. "Turn and face it."

If the Klingon heard, he gave no indication, and continued to sprint for the tree, eyeing a low-hanging branch.

Mourl meant to leap for it.

By now the *targ's* snarls were loud, even from Karel's position—more than two dozen meters away.

Mourl turned quickly and saw the *targ* nearly on top of him.

He couldn't wait another second. He leaped for the branch, putting all of his strength into that single burst…
…and missed.

He came down hard on the ground, stumbled forward, fell, and tried to immediately roll to his feet.

But the *targ* got there first. It hit the Klingon at full speed, its mouth tusks piercing Mourl in the side.

The Klingon howled and reached for his *mek'leth,* which hung from his side. Unfortunately, that side was pressed against the ground.

Without thinking, Karel was racing for his friend, sensing his brother behind him.

The *targ* backed away and bit hard into Mourl's hand. The Klingon howled again, using his good hand to push at the *targ,* leaving his head and throat unprotected.

The *targ* struck with great speed and bit straight into Mourl's throat. The screams stopped abruptly.

Karel forced himself to a stop and grabbed out to reach for his brother. He slowly began backing away. Mourl was beyond help. He had to make sure that Kell got home.

Quickly glancing around, Karel could see the backs of the other three of their group as they disappeared in the distance.

When he turned back, he saw that the targ did not mean to tarry on Mourl. Its head was turned up and it was watching Karel and Kell carefully.

Karel knew he had no choice but to face the *targ* directly.

"Keep moving back," he said forcefully to his brother. "If I fail, you will need some distance to escape."

Kell said nothing, but Karel heard his brother's footsteps behind him. He was pleased to see that his brother was showing some sense. He did not want to face his mother if he failed to bring down the *targ* and then failed to protect his brother.

Karel realized that if he did not bring down the *targ,* the animal would make certain he was spared the task of facing anyone. Karel grabbed his *mek'leth* firmly in hand and asked Kahless and the spirit of his father for the strength to prevail.

Then he heard the shouting behind him.

Snapping his head around, Karel saw his brother shouting and swinging his *mek'leth* back and forth to attract the *targ,* just as he would do if he were the apex of a pincer formation during a hunt.

The difference was that there weren't four other Klingons to weaken the beast before it reached him. And Kell was only eight years old and didn't have the size or strength to stop a *targ* at full charge.

Courage and determination were powerful weapons for a warrior, but they alone would not win a battle.

Karel began shouting himself, but the *targ* had seen Kell and was charging after him.

The pincer formation was effective because a charging *targ* would not stop until it had reached its target or had died. Thus, the Klingons on either side of the charging beast could strike blows at it.

When the *targ* swept past him, Karel acted without thinking and swung his *mek'leth* in a swift arc. He made satisfying contact with the beast's hide. The *targ* slowed slightly.

Another two or three blows like that and the *targ* might have actually been slowed and weakened enough to make a difference.

Kell stood firm, holding the *mek'leth* directly in front of him. Karel knew that Kell's best chance was to hold the sword high and swing it hard as the *targ* attacked him. Of course, given the circumstances, Karel knew that would make very little difference.

Still, Karel hoped that Kell would hurt the creature before it set on him.

The *targ* was just meters away now, but Kell still stood firm. Karel found himself yelling and noted that his brother was doing the same. It was a *Mok'bara* cry—a cry of battle.

Then the *targ* prepared to leap and Kell suddenly dropped, jamming his *mek'leth* into the ground. Even if the *targ* had seen the danger, it would not have been able to stop. The animal leapt, flying through the air for a brief moment until its chest hit the blade, which Kell held firm.

The *targ* kept moving, flying toward the hilt of the weapon, even as the blade tore through it.

By the time the beast had come to a rest, Karel was there, kneeling next to his brother.

Both the young Klingon and the beast were still. Kell could see they were connected. One of the *targ*'s tusks had burrowed deeply into Kell's shoulder.

Grabbing the *targ* around the neck, Karel pulled and the tusk came out. Tossing the beast aside, Karel watched as his brother's wound began to bleed freely. He turned his brother onto his back and felt for a pulse. He was relieved to find it strong.

Taking a quick look around, he saw that none of the others from their party was in sight. Grabbing Kell by the neck and knees, he lifted.

That was when the younger Klingon stirred.

"No," he whispered.

"What?" Karel asked, bringing his head closer to hear.

"No...I can walk," Kell said.

Karel put his brother down and thought it a wonder that Kell was standing. Yet Kell had taken a few shaky steps.

The two brothers made their way out of the woods. Finally, the younger Klingon allowed Karel to put a hand on his good arm and help him along.

As they reached the path leading home, Kell shook off even that small help. Karel watched in amazement as Kell straightened up and headed for home.

Karel woke up slowly in his bunk on the *D'k tahg*. As he opened his eyes, he felt a warmth that he had not known since he had last been home. He had just seen his brother....

Karel saw Kell's face, the face as it appeared in the

dream. Even as he saw it, the face began to recede and Karel remembered that Kell was dead.

He remembered.

The grief came, then the anger, then the fury.

The Earthers had taken his brother. The cowardly, deceitful Earthers. For a moment, his mind rebelled. It was not possible. Such sub-Klingons could not stop the warrior's heart that Kell had possessed. No mere Earther could cool his brother's blood.

Yet somehow they had. He was sure of that.

He was equally sure they would pay. Karel would make sure of it. Honor demanded it, and honor would be paid.

Chapter One

STARSHIP *U.S.S. ENTERPRISE*
FEDERATION SPACE

LESLIE PARRISH TRACED the scar on Kell's shoulder.

"What is that?" she asked.

"Just a scar," he said.

"Pretty nasty for *just a scar*," she said.

The Klingon leaned into her. She had no choice but to press back against him in the small bed.

"Mmmm," she said. "But we both have to be on duty in an hour. We'll have to get up now if we want to eat."

Kell grunted his displeasure, but knew she was right.

"How did you get it?" she asked.

"I was very young..." he said. "It was an accident."

"Farming accident?" she asked.

"Hmmm...yes, a farming accident," Kell said. It was a small lie, yet it pained Kell to tell it. Honor demanded truthfulness...and Leslie Parrish deserved it. They had

13

fought together and nearly died together. And they had become…close in the time since. Initially, he had fooled himself that their closeness was merely a reaction to the battle and victory they had shared.

Now he knew that was not true and would not utter the lie, even to himself. The truth in this case, however, did not provide clarity.

In this case, the truth was very dangerous to Kell, to his mission, and, finally, to her.

"I was eight," he said, needing to tell her something of the truth.

"Must have scared the hell out of your mother," she said.

"Nearly," he said.

Kell felt the scar himself. The Klingon surgeons who had transformed him into a human—at least on the outside—had offered to remove the scar.

He had refused, even though it might increase his danger, since the real Jon Anderson he was replacing had no such scar.

He needed something to remind him of who he was as he took the face of the sworn enemy of the Klingon Empire.

Kell turned to Parrish and pulled her close.

"Jon," she said, making his name a question.

"I think we should skip breakfast today," he said.

"Come in, Mr. Anderson," Section Chief Sam Fuller said. The Klingon did not hesitate. Through training and practice, he had learned to respond immediately to his assumed human name.

Kell entered the security office. His human commanding officer, Fuller, was sitting behind the desk, smiling warmly at him.

In Klingon Intelligence, he had found that a call to meet privately with a superior officer almost always meant an unpleasant encounter or a confrontation of some kind. He had found that this was not so for humans, at least the ones he had met in Starfleet.

For the first few days on the *Enterprise,* he had steeled himself every time someone called his human name, convinced that he would be denounced as a Klingon agent in the next breath. He was sure that someone would see him for what he was, an Infiltrator. He waited for someone to discover that he was *betleH 'etlh,* or the Blade of the *Bat'leth.*

It had not happened.

The humans were remarkably trusting of one another. Most Klingons would see that as a weakness, a fatal one that could be exploited. Kell knew this was not true. The humans he had met and served with trusted each other because they found each other worthy of trust.

In that case, the trust was not a weakness but a great strength, because when they fought, they fought as one.

Kell trusted the human behind the desk. He had fought with Sam Fuller. In any sane universe, they should have died in battle together. Yet they had survived and had won the day.

While Kell had seen many signs of Fuller's alien nature, he had seen the man's courage and his honor. That honor and courage were worthy of a true follower of Kahless.

Kell was certain that no Klingon would believe such a thing possible for a human. Yet it was true and Kell would not deny it.

"Sit down, Ensign," Fuller said, gesturing to the chair facing his desk.

Taking a seat, Kell studied the human's features. In his less than two weeks aboard the *Enterprise,* he had become adept at reading human expressions and body language.

He could see that Chief Fuller had something serious to discuss with him.

"Ensign, it's now been almost two weeks since the incident in System 1324," Fuller said. "How are you feeling?"

"I am fine, Chief," Kell replied. "How are *you* feeling? Your injuries are healing?"

Fuller waved his hand dismissively. "Good as new."

Yet Kell could see that was not true. The chief's movements were slower and more deliberate since the incident. His smashed ribs and punctured lung had obviously not healed completely.

"I want to talk to you about your future," Fuller continued.

"My future?" Kell asked, wondering how Fuller would react if he knew just how short the Klingon expected that future to be.

"I have spoken to the captain and he wanted me to have this discussion with all the survivors of the incident." Fuller paused for just a moment, studying him carefully. "Starfleet is offering an honorable discharge to any of the survivors who would like it."

"A discharge?" the Klingon asked.

"You all served well and seceded in your mission. You also saw more death in one day than most people who serve in Starfleet see in a career."

The Klingon shook his head.

"That is not necessary, sir," Kell said.

"Don't be so hasty, Ensign. I want you to think about this. You are a decorated officer in Starfleet who is being given a chance to return to civilian life with full honors. No one would think less of you if you wanted to do something else with your life. You have done your part and then some."

The Klingon shook his head again.

"Son, you have to think about this, that's an order. And it comes directly from Captain Kirk."

The sound of Kirk's name made Kell pause. In the Empire, Kirk was known as a treacherous and deceitful coward, a great betrayer. It was not true, the Klingon now knew.

Kirk was honorable and had courage. He had risked his own life to rescue the lowest-ranking officers on his ship—the security team trapped in the caves on the second planet of System 1324.

He had also saved Kell's life.

But as an Infiltrator, it was the Klingon's first duty to kill Captain Kirk.

"I have thought about it, sir. I cannot leave the service," Kell said.

"Sorry, Ensign, you have to give it more thought than that. We will be putting in to the starbase in less than two days. We will be there for at least a few days to take on supplies and...replacement crew. You have until we set out again from the starbase to give me your answer. You *will* use that time and you will give this issue serious thought. And that is an order."

The Klingon nodded, and for a moment he did think about it. Since he had arrived on the *Enterprise*, he had been certain that he would die on this mission. The prospect of his death did not trouble him when he believed he was serving the Empire in the defeat of its enemies.

But humans were not what he had expected. And now he owed Captain Kirk an honor debt. To kill the human meant Kell would forfeit his honor. Still, his duty to the Empire demanded it.

Yet here was a way out. He could accept the discharge and leave the ship. Then just disappear into the Federation. Even if he did decide to let Kirk live, he could not avoid eventually being exposed as a Klingon on the *Enterprise.*

If he were injured on a mission, a routine medical scan would reveal him instantly. And he had seen that security officers were very prone to injury in the course of their duties.

Even if he somehow managed to avoid injury, he would not be able to avoid the next routine physical, which was just a few short months away.

Now Fuller had offered him something he did not think was possible: a way out. He could escape with his honor intact.

Yet even as the thought struck him, he knew he would not do it. He would not abandon his people, to wander the Federation while the inevitable conflict between the Klingon Empire and Federation drew near. He would serve the Empire as his brother served it on a Klingon battle cruiser, as their father had served it twenty-five years ago in battle against Starfleet.

He would do his duty and face the consequences to his honor.

"I will think about it, Chief," Kell said as he stood up.

Fuller seemed satisfied with that and stood to shake Kell's hand.

"Thank you, Ensign," he said.

The Klingon nodded and turned to go, but a sudden thought stopped him.

"Chief, did the captain make the same offer to you?" he asked.

"Yes, he did," Fuller said.

"What was your answer?" Kell asked.

The chief paused for a moment, then said, "I agreed to think about it."

The Klingon did not doubt that was true. Yet looking into Fuller's eyes, he was certain that the section chief had also already made up his mind.

After Sam Fuller entered the briefing room and took his seat, Captain Kirk nodded to the assembled officers in the briefing room. All of the department heads were there, as well as all of the security section chiefs—all of the *surviving* security section chiefs, Kirk reminded himself. Section Chief Ordover and twelve other officers had died on the second planet of System 1324.

"I have just spoken to Admiral Justman and about the incident with the Orion vessels. The Orion government initially denied that any such incident occurred. When confronted by the overwhelming evidence that Security Chief Giotto collected on the planet and this ship's own logs, Orion officials questioned the accuracy of the evidence and finally allowed that the incident in System 1324 may have happened, but if it did it was the action of private Orion citizens, with no affiliation to the Orion government."

"Poppycock," McCoy groused.

"On the contrary, Doctor," Spock countered. "Most Orion privateers operate independently, without the sanction of any Orion political organization. They are, essentially, businessmen."

"The question is, what was their business in System 1324? They attacked a small, unarmed settlement with nothing of real value. Then they took on our security force and this ship," Kirk said. "Ideas, anyone?"

There was a brief silence, which McCoy broke. "If no one else is going to say it, I will, Captain. They were clearly hired by the Klingons to engage a starship and Starfleet personnel on the ground to gather intelligence about our capabilities."

Kirk smiled. McCoy had vocalized what everyone in the room was thinking. The theory fit all the facts and was especially compelling in the light of the recent security warning from Starfleet command.

"I agree with the doctor," Spock said. "Unfortunately, we have no evidence of such a connection. And without the cooperation of the Orion government, it will be nearly impossible to establish."

"What does Starfleet say, Captain?" McCoy asked.

"Officially, there is no proof of Klingon involvement in the incident, or of any connection between the Klingon government and private Orion *businessmen*," Kirk said.

McCoy was already shaking his head.

Kirk spoke before the doctor could voice his thoughts. "Unofficially, finding such a connection has become a high priority for all active starships. We are to actively scan for any unusual Orion activity."

"Captain, what will that accomplish?" Scotty said.

"We already know the Klingons are preparing for war. Even if we prove the Klingons and Orions are working together, we'll still be looking at the same larger problem."

"Quite right, Mr. Scott," Kirk said. "But we need to shut down any Orion intelligence-gathering operations before information reaches the Klingon Empire. We are also to use all available means to learn about the Klingon plans from any hostile Orion forces we encounter."

"Aye," Scott said, "I just hope that the Klingons will nae slip in the back door while we are chasing Orions."

As Kirk nodded, McCoy spoke again.

"Can we inform the crew of this mission, Captain?" the doctor asked.

Kirk shook his head. "No, right now the Klingon situation is still classified. We are under orders to keep it from becoming general knowledge." Kirk raised his hand to silence the doctor's protest. "To give the diplomats more maneuvering room in dealing with the Klingons."

Kirk turned to his Vulcan first officer. "Mr. Spock, please begin scanning for relevant signs of unusual activity."

"Yes, sir," Spock said. "However, it will be a difficult task given the varied nature of Orion...activities in the galaxy."

"Noted," Kirk said. "Lieutenant Uhura, coordinate with Command to allocate some of your resources to study Orion communications and codes."

"Yes, sir," the communications officer replied.

"Mr. Scott, status of repairs."

"All repairs complete, Captain," the chief engineer said. "We have replaced or repaired all of the artificial-gravity generators, as well as all affected circuits. We also upgraded a few systems. Additional repairs at starbase will nae be necessary."

"But a checkout by starbase personnel is required by regulations since some of the repairs were supposed to be performed at starbase facilities."

"Captain—" Scotty began.

"Regulations, sorry, Mr. Scott. I will speak to the base commander and make sure the starbase engineers are out of your engine room as quickly as possible."

Mr. Scott seemed satisfied.

"Time to Starbase 42, Mr. Spock?" Kirk asked.

"One day, four hours, forty-one minutes, Captain," the Vulcan said without even checking his computer terminal.

"Shore-leave schedule for the crew?" Kirk asked.

"Completed, Captain," Spock said.

"Excellent," Kirk said, standing. "Thank you for your time."

Chapter Two

STARFLEET COMMAND HEADQUARTERS
SAN FRANCISCO, EARTH

LIEUTENANT WEST entered the admiral's office, carrying his data padd. The admiral gave him a warm smile and gestured to the seat in front of his desk.

West took the seat, which gave him a full view of the San Francisco Bay and the Golden Gate, which dominated the large window behind the admiral.

When West had first entered that office, he had been impressed by the view in spite of himself. Now, he still thought the view powerful and beautiful, but West's galaxy had changed since then.

At first, he had seen it as a metaphor for the power that Admiral Justman and Starfleet commanded. Now, it was a symbol of what the Federation stood to lose—*would* lose if what the admiral feared came to pass.

"I have prepared my report, Admiral," West said.

"Give me the highlights," the admiral said.

"I have looked at every piece of Klingon cultural information I could find, going all the way back to the earliest entries in the Vulcan database. The most promising line of inquiry I found was regarding a growing cult around the Klingon religious warrior figure named Kahless, who lived fifteen hundred years ago. His teaching codified many of the Klingon cultural beliefs about honor and personal behavior. While still an aggressive philosophy, it provides a framework of rules, an understanding of which in the future could be an asset in negotiations."

"In the future?" the admiral asked.

West was no longer surprised by the admiral's ability to see right to the heart of any complex issue.

"As I said, the cult is growing, but is not yet a dominant force in the Empire. I do not think that will happen for another seventy-five to one hundred years," West said. "It's in nothing we can use for the current crisis. I'm sorry, sir."

The admiral merely nodded.

Back at the Academy, West had believed that modern cultural-analysis techniques would make warfare a thing of the past. As a xenoanthropologist, West was prepared to do pioneering work in that field himself.

He had expected to do that work on a starship, over the course of years. Instead, the admiral had made him a special adjunct and given him an office at Starfleet Command. The admiral had also given him virtually unlimited resources to come up with a peaceful solution to the current problems with the Klingon Empire.

"I do have a list of suggestions and possible strategies for Ambassador Fox and his team," West said. "They may be helpful in negotiations."

The admiral studied West for a moment, then said, "But nothing that will likely forestall the current crisis."

"No, sir," West said.

The admiral read something in his face. "Son, you have been on this project for less than two weeks. I expect the best from everyone on my staff, but I don't expect miracles."

West knew that two weeks was barely enough time to scratch the surface of a project of this scope, with stakes this high. But that was an excuse and West knew it. Two years of study would not yield him better results.

The lieutenant had made a name for himself at the Academy as an outsider. He had gained a certain notoriety for his papers criticizing Starfleet policy for being too quick to rely on military solutions to problems that could have been solved with cultural understanding and diplomacy.

Those views had cost West friends and his relationship with his father. Now, he had the ear of a fleet admiral, who West firmly believed wanted a peaceful solution to the Klingon problem. And all West had to offer were negotiating tips and excuses.

"I'm...sorry, sir."

Admiral Justman showed genuine surprise for a moment. Then he gave West a thin smile.

"You are nothing to apologize for, Mr. West. In fact, I owe *you* an apology," Justman said.

"Sir?" West said, not bothering to mask his own surprise.

"I read your work on the importance of xenostudies in the management of relations with other races. I knew it was an overdue to play a more important role in what we do," Justman said.

"And you brought me here, gave me everything I asked for," West said.

"Knowing all the time that I was asking you to do the impossible—to do what teams of xenostudies personnel in the diplomatic corps had failed to do. I asked you to stop a war that is almost certainly inevitable."

The admiral raised a hand to silence West's protest.

"And I have to admit that I took some pleasure in opening your eyes to the realities we face here. That was one of the reasons I choose you in particular for this job. It was beneath me and beneath the service," Justman said.

West did not know what to say. Of all the things that the admiral had said and done to surprise him, that apology was the most surprising of all.

Yet it did not erase a milligram of the shame that he felt at his own failure.

West said nothing for a long moment. Finally, the admiral broke the silence. "Let's hope we live long enough to study our regrets, Lieutenant."

Returning the admiral's smile, West was suddenly struck by something the admiral had said.

"What were the other reasons you chose me, Admiral?" West asked.

For a moment, West thought he had caught the admiral by surprise. Then, he heard the door open behind him.

Turning, West saw a male yeoman enter carrying a large tray. West was disappointed that it was not Yeoman Hatcher. She was attractive and he had been meaning to find a moment to speak to her alone.

The yeoman put the tray down on the small conference table by the window.

"I took the liberty," the admiral said, getting up.

West took his customary seat and was not surprised to see one of his favorite foods on the plate in front of him.

After they were done eating, the admiral said, "Tell me what you have. We have a meeting with Ambassador Fox tomorrow. After the last time you and he spoke, I expect him to be on his guard."

West spoke for the next hour, with the admiral asking pointed questions. The information was not much, but it would provide some advantage in negotiations. And in the current situation, he knew that Starfleet and the diplomatic corps needed all the advantage they could muster.

It was only later, back at his desk, that West realized the admiral had not answered his question about why he was hired.

Kell exited the turbolift and headed toward his destination. He did not hurry. He was not looking forward to his duty, but he knew he must do it. The Klingon knew he had waited too long—and that time had made the task harder, not easier.

And the longer he waited, the harder it would become. And the greater the chance of his own exposure.

As he stood outside the door, he found himself hesitating to take the next step, the one that would lead him inside. Less than two weeks ago, he had faced down an overwhelming force of Orions and their weapons. He had not hesitated or flinched from his duty then.

Yet he hesitated now. It was not fear, he knew—at

least, not exactly. It was a reluctance to hurt humans that he had come to respect—humans to whom he owed his life.

Nevertheless, his duty to the Empire was clear and he would do it without concern for how he felt about his actions. In many ways, his task would be a kindness that prevented further loss and pain.

Stepping forward, the Klingon watched the door open. Leslie Parrish was inside.

"Jon," she said, her face immediately brightening.

The Klingon nodded and entered the quarters. His face was set.

"What is it?" she asked, concern in her voice.

For a moment he did not know how to begin.

"What's wrong?" she prodded, touching him gently on the shoulder.

By force of will, he opened his mouth and said, "I wish to speak with you."

She smiled at that. "You *wish* to speak. That's a first. I don't know anyone who avoids conversation more."

Her smile faded when she saw that his own serious expression was not changing.

"We have become close," he said. Then, for a moment, he was unable to think of anything else to say.

"That is one way to put it," she said in a flat voice without any of her previous humor.

"I have...valued that closeness. But I do not see a possibility for a long-term...situation for us," he said.

Leslie's face had set and was unreadable. "Have I asked you for a *long-term situation?*"

Kell did not know how to respond to that. He suspected she did not expect a literal answer.

"Have I?" she demanded.

"No," he replied, giving the only answer he could think of.

By her expression, he could see that the answer did not please her.

"Then what are we talking about!" she shouted.

The Klingon knew he had to try a different approach.

"It is just that this is dangerous for us," he said.

"What is dangerous? Our *closeness,* the fact that we might face a *long-term situation,* or that fact that every day either of us might beam down to a planet and not beam back up?"

The answer was yes to all of those things, and to other questions she did not and could not ask. However, the Klingon felt sure that another literal answer would just anger her further.

"Well?" she demanded. "I'm waiting—"

"Leslie," he said. Kell rarely addressed her by her first name, and it stopped her in midsentence. For a moment, her face softened.

"Everyone's afraid of getting close," she said. "I think it's worse in our job because of what we face every day. That's why we have to have more courage than everyone else." Then she gave him a thin smile. "After all, risk is our business."

The Klingon returned the smile. He didn't know how to tell her that what was difficult for most human security officers was completely impossible for him. That while others might have a slim chance at having a long-term situation, such a situation was not only impossible for him, but also dangerous for her.

Then he realized that he was doing what he was doing *for her*. It would protect her, her life, and her feelings.

His own feelings were too strong to allow any kind of harm to come to her if he could prevent it.

He could tell her none of this, just as he could not tell her the truth of his birth and his blood.

No, he could not tell her the truth. Instead, he just looked at her, trying to communicate with his eyes what he could not put into words of any language. He willed to her what he felt, he willed to her his conflict and his pain and what he had to do.

He hoped that somehow, she might understand.

For a long moment, the silence hung in the air between them. Finally, he spoke. "I cannot continue to see you."

He watched understanding wash over her face. Perhaps not understanding, but acceptance. Then her face set, in a way that he had not seen since the incident on the second planet of System 1324. Her expression should have warned him of what would come next, but the blow came too quickly for that. Leslie Parrish struck out with her right hand, bringing the palm flatly against his face.

For a moment, he was too stunned by the slap to closely follow what happened next. She was shouting and pushing at him.

A moment later, she gave him a hard shove that sent him into the corridor. He struck a technician who was walking by and nearly sent the man sprawling.

"Get out!" He heard the shout one last time before the doors to her quarters closed.

The Klingon turned to make sure the human he had struck was unharmed.

"It's okay," the man said, looking at him with understanding.

For a moment the others passing by in the corridor glanced at Kell with embarrassed sympathy and then continued on their way.

Chapter Three

LIEUTENANT WEST and Admiral Justman were the first to arrive at the diplomatic briefing. The first time West had seen the conference room, he had been a first-year cadet and he had been impressed by its size and the view of the bay. The second time was just two weeks ago, and he had accompanied the admiral on only his second day on the job. He had been worried then about the future and the coming conflict with the Klingons, yet he had been hopeful and determined to help prevent that terrible outcome.

This time, he was still determined but less hopeful.

The admiral's staff arrived and West noted that they treated him with respect. He knew he had impressed them in the last diplomatic briefing. He also knew they believed in his project because the admiral did.

He wished he felt worthy of that confidence.

The ambassador and his staff entered, exchanged polite greetings with the admiral and his officers. At the first meeting, West had seen the ambassador's confident stride and bearing as arrogant and self-important.

Since then, West had studied the ambassador's record. He had prevented major wars, saved countless lives.

West had been pleased to show off his own insights into dealing with the Klingons. He had enjoyed embarrassing the ambassador.

West felt shame run through him. A lot had changed in two weeks. *He* had changed.

And so, apparently, had Ambassador Fox.

There were creases in the man's face that West was sure had not been there last time. He had the haunted look of a man who carried a heavy burden. West knew that look, because he had seen it on Admiral Justman's face.

The ambassador faced him and the lieutenant saw something that shocked him—a bandage on the man's forehead. Suddenly, West was certain that Fox had received the injury under that bandage in negotiation with his Klingon counterpart.

Ambassador Fox was looking at him expectantly before West realized the man had addressed him. He also noted that the ambassador's staff was scowling at him.

"Hello, Ambassador," West said.

Fox nodded and turned to take his seat.

"Ambassador," West said, "I would like to apologize for my behavior at the last meeting."

Fox looked at him with genuine surprise. "Apologize?"

"I was out of line, sir," West said.

The ambassador dismissed him with a wave. "You were right. Never apologize when you are right, Lieutenant."

West took his own seat. "Your insights helped us secure the first meeting I have had with the Klingon ambassador in months."

"Was the meeting productive?" Admiral Justman asked.

"Illuminating, Admiral," Fox responded. "But, no. It was not productive. We made some progress on trade agreements and other small matters, but the Klingon ambassador refused to discuss or even acknowledge any significant problems between the Empire and the Federation. I finally questioned him directly about the Klingon arms buildup and fleet maneuvers and he refused to budge from his position. Of course he was lying."

"You are sure?" Justman said.

"Absolutely, I can tell when I am being lied to by a practiced and accomplished equivocator. The Klingon ambassador is neither practiced nor accomplished. I am convinced that the Empire is preparing for war, a war they will wage in approximately seven months."

"Seven months?" West said, gasping.

"Seven months," Fox repeated, his voice strong and confident.

"Are you sure of the time frame? Intelligence reports have provided us with a range—"

"Seven months," the ambassador repeated. "It coincides with the time frame for all of the important concession and compromise points that the Klingon ambassador made. I am certain the ambassador was lying and has no intention of honoring those commitments because he and the Klingon Council believe we will be at war by then."

A heavy silence descended over the table.

"My next discussion with the Klingon ambassador needs to be much more frank, Admiral. My question for you is, how prepared is Starfleet for a Klingon attack of the kind we are facing?"

The admiral did not hesitate. "We are not ready," he said.

Fox simply nodded. "In seven months?"

"We will be more ready," Justman said.

"But not completely," the ambassador finished for him.

"No," the admiral said. "Starfleet is basically a civilian organization. We were lucky when the *Enterprise* repelled the recent Romulan incursion. And we've been fortunate that the Federation has not faced a serious large-scale threat to its security in fifteen years. The Klingons have been preparing for this fight for twenty-five years. The bottom line is that if they attack today, we lose. In seven months we have a chance."

West did not have to ask how good a chance. He had read the intelligence reports on the Klingon buildup and he knew enough about Starfleet resources to guess the rest.

"We would have an even better chance if the Klingons would wait another four or five years," Justman said. "The next-generation starship is in development now."

Ambassador Fox gave a grim smile. "I will keep that in mind."

Fox studied the table for a moment. "Seven months is still a long time, and nothing is inevitable. Getting a meeting with the Klingons was a small victory. We will simply have to do better and convince the Klingons they have nothing to gain from an attack. Mr. West, I understand you have a new report on possible negotiation strategies."

West nodded. "I agree with you, Ambassador, that the key is to convince the Klingons that they can't win, that in fact they would suffer a humiliating defeat. The key concepts are the Klingon notions of duty and honor."

For the next hour West spoke. To his own ears, his conclusions seemed pitifully thin, but the ambassador listened carefully and asked pointed questions, as did his staff.

For a brief moment, West found himself believing that Fox might indeed be able to work a miracle and that his own work would help in some small way.

He and the admiral walked back to their offices together.

"Have you seen the report from the *Enterprise?*" Justman asked.

"Yes, sir. The incident was terrible," West replied. The lieutenant felt a pang at the mention of the *Enterprise.* He had requested that vessel as his first choice for starship service. That was before the admiral had sidetracked the career he had planned for himself.

It was less than two weeks ago, yet it felt like a lifetime.

"What do you think of Captain Kirk's conclusions that the operation was an attempt by the Orions to collect intelligence on starship capabilities and Starfleet ground-force tactics?" the admiral said.

West thought before he answered. The captain's conclusions were completely unsubstantiated. They fit the events and the facts, but there was no proof. It was exactly the kind of military thinking that West had objected to so much in his days at the academy.

"I think Captain Kirk is absolutely right," Lieutenant West replied.

If the admiral was surprised by his response, the older man did not show it.

"I do as well," Justman said as he entered his own outer office.

West turned and headed into his own office. Sitting at his desk, he prepared himself for a long night. Or more precisely, he prepared himself for seven months of long nights. In his washroom, he splashed water on his face.

Looking in the mirror, he saw something that surprised him—a haunted expression on the face of the young lieutenant who looked back at him.

Karel found something like peace in his disruptor room. Focusing on his job had allowed him to focus the fury caused by the Earthers who had taken his father years ago and now his brother.

Every time the port disruptors fired, he imagined they burned with the vengeance of the Klingon Empire as his blood burned with it.

He also took pride in the performance of the weapons room. It had improved significantly since he had replaced Gash as the commander. In the days since that time, he had only faced a single challenge to his command.

Karel believed that the reason the others had not challenged him yet was because his leadership had gotten results. The port disruptor room was not only more efficient than it had been, it was now performing better than the starboard disruptor room—much better. That might cause Karel a problem later with the senior weapons officer there, but Karel would worry about that when the time came.

For now, he saw that he had given pride to the Klingons he commanded. Kahless taught that a warrior fought best when his blood was tested and put to good use.

On the other hand, Karel had seen that Klingons often—too often—put their ambitions ahead of their duty. He did not dare allow himself to lower his guard because he perceived that his Klingons respected him. If he did, he would end up like Gash, who had lost an eye and his command to Karel's challenge.

As the final drill of the day ended, Karel surveyed the results, visiting each weapons console and giving praise and corrections as necessary. He was impressed by Torg's performance. Karel had had to break the Klingon's hand when the Klingon had tended Karel's backup cooling system. The hand was healing and Torg had done particularly well. It was a short time ago that Torg had tried to sabotage Karel's work for his own advancement. Now the Klingon was offering suggestions for improvement to the junior officer who ran the backup system next to him.

As Karel was about to call the end of the duty cycle and release the officers to seek out their evening *gagh,* he heard the doors to the disruptor room open. The senior weapons officer and his crew had arrived for the next duty cycle.

They took their positions and Karel dismissed his own Klingons. He saw the senior officer looking at him, sizing him up, and made a note to himself to be wary of trouble from the officer. As the day officer, Karel held the superior position. A challenge was inevitable.

Karel watched as his Klingons left the disruptor room. After the last one was gone, Karel followed, and was immediately met by two warriors in the corridor.

"Come," the largest of them said.

"What do you want?" Karel spat back.

"The commander wants you in his quarters," he said.

Karel knew this moment would come. In face, he was surprised it had not come sooner.

Nodding, he headed for the weapons commander's quarters, *ahead* of the two guards. Karel sensed the Klingons behind him bristling at the insult but he was determined to seek out his own fate—he would not be led to it.

Once there, he entered the commander's quarters without hesitation, every muscle alert and ready for movement. Karel noted with relief that the commander's guards stayed outside. Clearly, the Klingon was prepared to handle Karel himself.

Inside, the commander was on his feet and waiting for him. Though Karel had of course seen the Klingon on the ship, they had not met face-to-face since Karel's promotion to senior weapons officer. As the bridge weapons officer, the commander was in charge of both disruptor rooms and answered only to Second Officer Klak and the captain.

"Senior Weapons Officer Karel," the commander said, appraising him.

"Commander," Karel said, meeting the other Kling-on's gaze.

"Sit," the commander said, pointing to a seat.

But Karel's father had sired no fools. He would not give that advantage to his superior. "I will stand."

Then the commander did something Karel did not expect. He smiled.

"As you wish," he said, taking a seat opposite Karel.

Was the commander insulting him? Baiting him? Karel decided to wait to see his next move.

"You went to Second Officer Klak for information," the commander said.

"Yes," Karel said.

"It was a great insult to your superior Gash," the commander said.

"It was intended as an insult. Gash was a fool and had failed to act on my simple request. I had no choice but to go over his head," Karel said.

The commander nodded. "Gash was a fool. I would have replaced him soon if one of his subordinates had not done the job for me. You have done that, but you have left me with a new problem."

Karel waited for what would come now.

"Did you intend to insult me as well?" the commander asked.

It was a direct question and deserved a direct response. "No," Karel said.

"Yet you did not come to me. You went to my superior," the commander said.

"The second officer's contacts and…access to information are well known," Karel said. "I needed immediate results."

"You wanted news of your brother," the commander said.

Karel nodded.

"Your brother had an impressive record in intelligence. He served the Empire well," the commander said.

For a moment, Karel was not sure if the Klingon was baiting him. Both Gash and Second Officer Klak had looked down on Kell's service in intelligence—most Klingons looked at noncombatant service the same way.

But the commander's face showed no signs of falsehood.

"A warrior like Second Officer Klak who trades in information can accomplish much without showing his face," the commander said.

"Only an enemy without honor refuses to show his face in battle," Karel countered, quoting Kahless.

"You believe this?" the commander said.

"It is a truth whether or not I believe it," Karel replied.

The commander held his gaze for a long moment. "Do you wish to challenge me?" he said.

"No," Karel said. "Not now."

"Why not?" the commander asked.

"Because I fight the enemies of the Empire," Karel said.

"But what about your ambitions?" the commander said.

"I have one ambition, Commander: to crush our enemies," Karel said.

"Earthers?" the commander said.

"Yes, Earthers. They killed my father at Donatu V and now my brother in a cowardly attack. I can best make them pay from my position in the disruptor room," Karel said.

"But to do that you will first have to leave this room alive," the commander said, standing up.

The commander stood up and leaned closer to Karel.

"One of your officers challenged you already. I watched the surveillance records. You let him live, why?"

"He was a good officer, experienced. I needed him in the disruptor room," Karel said.

"Do *I* need *you?*" the commander said.

"I serve the Empire. Its enemies are my enemies," Karel said.

The commander backed away slightly. "If you challenge me again, in any way, you will become my enemy. And then you will die. Do you understand?"

"Yes, Commander Koloth," Karel said.

Chapter Four

"WHY THE CLOAK AND DAGGER, Jim?" McCoy asked.

Kirk stepped onto the transporter. "I don't know, Bones, but the commodore was very clear. No shore leave for the crew until we meet."

Spock took his place on the transporter pad next to Kirk.

For a moment, the doctor lingered on the deck. Kirk raised an eyebrow and, frowning, McCoy stepped up to the platform.

When he was in place, Kirk said to the technician, "Energize, Mr. Kyle."

The transporter beam deposited them on a transporter platform on the starbase. To Kirk's surprise, they were met by Commodore Krinsky himself. Kirk had never met the man before, but knew him by reputation.

As the commodore walked, his limp betrayed the injury that had forced him from active service on a starship.

"Hello, Captain," the commodore said as he shook Kirk's hand.

"Commodore," Kirk said, "this is my first officer, Mr. Spock, and my chief medical officer, Dr. McCoy."

Krinsky's face was all business. He nodded to Spock and McCoy, then turned back to Kirk.

"What is their security clearance?" he asked.

"Top level," Kirk replied.

"Very well, come with me. I have Admiral Justman waiting for you on our com system," he said, leading them out of the room.

In the corridor, Kirk asked, "Why not just contact me directly on the *Enterprise*'s system?"

"The admiral insisted on some extra security precautions. There are new codes. The code keys were hand-delivered yesterday. I have the new keys on data tapes to take back to your ship. But for now, the only secure station is in here," the commodore said, pointing to a door that was marked COMMUNICATIONS ROOM.

Then Krinsky raised his hand. "I'm afraid your people will have to wait out here. The admiral will tell you what you can share with them later."

Nodding, Kirk entered the room. The room was not large and was dominated by consoles on three sides. A single workstation sat in the center.

Kirk sat. The admiral's face was already on the screen. His expression was grim.

"Admiral Justman," Kirk said.

"Captain Kirk," the admiral responded. "I wish we were speaking under better circumstances. The situation is grave, Captain. I have just met with the diplomatic team working with the Klingons. Though diplomatic efforts will be ongoing, we have a revised timetable for the Klingon attack. Seven months."

"Is that confirmed?" Kirk asked.

"No, Jim. It is the ambassador's best guess, but I believe it to be accurate," Justman said.

Kirk nodded. That was enough for him. No one would ever get rich betting against the admiral's judgment.

"Does the ambassador see any hope?" Kirk asked.

"There's always hope, Captain, and seven months is not tomorrow. However, it will be a long and difficult road."

"What can the *Enterprise* do?" Kirk asked.

"Starfleet's focus now is to follow up on the Orion connection. It is our best chance for information within Federation space."

Kirk nodded. "Understood. Sir, why the additional security for this communication? We have all of the secure codes on the *Enterprise*. No new ones have appeared on the canceled list."

"We have had additional problems. There have been more security breaches that we cannot trace. More disappearances and some unexplained deaths. For now, we will no longer transmit new codes via subspace, even using cleared codes. Use only the codes you received from the commodore for secure communications. Frankly, Jim, we don't know what's secure anymore and what isn't. The Klingons already know more than they should about Starfleet operations. Our best chance to turn that around is by following the Orion trail," Justman said.

"The *Enterprise* will do everything it can, sir," Kirk said.

"I know that, Captain. You and your crew have never given less than exceptional efforts and extraordinary results." For a moment, the admiral's face softened. "I'm sorry about the people you lost in the 1324 incident, Jim."

"Thank you sir, they were good people," Kirk replied.

The admiral nodded, "We've lost too many good people."

Justman was silent for a moment, letting that statement hang in the air for a moment.

"I have instructed Commodore Krinsky to facilitate your departure. Make necessary repairs, but I have waived starbase engineering checks on your field repairs. I leave checks to your discretion and the discretion of your chief engineer. Resupply and make use of the starbase facilities, but get back out there quickly."

"How secure is what you have just told me?" Kirk asked.

"Share this information on a need-to-know basis only. Only with the people who absolutely must know and the ones you rely on most. Good luck, Captain Kirk. Justman out."

The screen went dark. Kirk stared at it for a moment before he got up and met Spock and McCoy.

The doctor took a look at his face and said, "What is it, Jim?"

Kirk told him. When he was finished, he said, "Mr. Spock, we need to call a meeting of the department heads immediately and we need to begin liberty for the crew. We will not have much time before we get under way again."

As Admiral Justman broke the connection he stood up and walked to the window that dominated two walls of his office. James Kirk was a good officer, a good man. There were just twelve men like him in the service— twelve captains of *starships*.

Those twelve men and those twelve ships had accomplished much in the twenty-five years of the starship program. Even if Justman failed in his mission to prevent the coming war, they would do what they had to in the coming months. They would each do their share— and more, Justman had no doubt.

Justman hoped that would somehow be enough.

The view from his office was of the San Francisco Bay and the Golden Gate Bridge. It was spectacular, but Admiral Justman did not see it. He was light-years away and twenty-five years in the past.

Lieutenant Robert Justman checked the weapons console in front of him. Phasers were online and photon torpedoes were armed and ready to fire. Shields were one hundred percent.

"All systems ready, sir," he said.

Captain Rodriguez said, "Acknowledged. Mr. Okuda, time to Donatu system?"

The science officer checked his computer and said, "Four minutes, sir."

The captain and the bridge crew waited. Justman checked and rechecked his data. The answer was the same with each repetition.

Time crawled by on the bridge.

Finally, Lieutenant Commander Okuda announced, "Approaching system now, sir."

"Helm," the captain said. "Take us to sublight on my mark. I want to come out of warp behind Donatu V. Let's not announce ourselves until we are ready."

Justman watched the screen change and felt the subtle vibration of the deck as the ship dropped out of warp.

"Full impulse to the Donatu V," the captain said.

Suddenly the blue-green planet dominated the viewscreen.

"Sensors, Mr. Okuda?" Captain Rodriguez said.

"I'm reading debris, and radiation in space," Okuda said, studying his viewer. "Sir…there was a warp-core breach here in the last few hours."

There was silence on the bridge as everyone absorbed that information.

"The colony?" the captain asked.

"No damage to the settlements that I can see," the science officer replied.

"I am reading multiple distress calls from the surface, as well as the *Endeavor*'s automated distress signal," the communications officer said.

"Maintain communications silence," the captain said. "Status on the *Endeavor?*"

"I'm reading something that might be the *Endeavor,* sir. And two other vessels. Klingon battle cruisers," Okuda said.

Justman tried to call up the ships on his tactical display. But the same planet that shielded the *Yorkshire* from the Klingon ships, made a tactical lock difficult.

And the background radiation was wreaking havoc with scanners.

"Eliminate magnification and bring us in close to the planet," the Captain ordered.

The view returned to normal and the planet grew in the center of the screen.

"Debris field up ahead," science officer Okuda said.

"Let's see it," the captain replied.

The view switched to a close view of the space above the planet's north pole. At first, the debris looked like a cloud. Then, as magnification increased, Justman was able to make out what looked like pieces of a hull. The lieutenant said a silent prayer that it was not pieces of the *Endeavor*.

Finally, he saw something he recognized and his stomach dropped. It was the largest piece of debris, cigar-shaped. It was unmistakable. They were looking at the front half of the nacelle of a Starfleet warp vessel, of the *Endeavor*.

No one on the bridge said a word, but Justman knew that everyone had seen the same thing and had come to the same conclusion. The ship had been wholly or partly destroyed. In all likelihood, the *Yorkshire* was now Donatu V's only defense.

"Time until the other Starfleet ships begin arriving?" Rodriguez said.

"The first will be here in three hours, forty-seven minutes," Okuda said. "I am also reading two more ships on long-range sensors. They are coming from Klingon space, sir."

"Keep scanning, Mr. Okuda. Apprise me of any changes," the captain said.

The captain's voice was steady. Justman knew it had more to do with Rodriguez's personal confidence than with their chances at the moment. Nonetheless, the even tones relaxed him.

Captain Rodriguez had gotten them out of tight spots before and won a number of impossible victories. If anyone could do that today, it was the captain.

"Status of shield, Mr. Justman," the captain asked.

"Full power," Justman said, trying to keep his own voice as steady as the captain's.

"We cannot let them get a foothold on the planet's surface," Rodriguez said. "Helm, bring us up above the North Pole. It's time we face the Klingons."

The captain turned to the communications officer. "Wait until they can see us and then begin hailing the Klingon vessels," he said.

Justman watched the main viewscreen, which was still trained on the debris field. He saw something float into the frame, turning end over end. In the instant before the view shifted to their direction of travel, he made out what the new piece of debris was—a body, or most of one. The image held for less than a second, but Justman could see that the Starfleet officer had been male and was still wearing his duty uniform.

The lieutenant could not make out the expression on the man's face, but he could imagine it—he could imagine it very well.

Chapter Five

KELL SAT AT HIS DESK and paged through the *Starfleet Survival Guide,* the copy that had belonged to the human he had replaced. He scanned each page, but the words ran together. It didn't matter; he had the book memorized. In any case, the activity was only a ruse in case his roommate walked in and asked him to beam over to the starbase.

The Klingon checked the time on the computer, and saw that it was almost time for Benitez to begin liberty. With any luck, Benitez would be on his way to the transporter room already.

Kell had barely finished the thought when Benitez walked in. The human took one look at him and said, "Come on, Flash, liberty begins in five minutes."

Shaking his head, the Klingon said, "I am reading."

Benitez looked at the book. "You've read that a hundred times. This is liberty, *on a starbase.* Haven't you heard? It might be the last time we get off the ship for a long time."

Then the human lowered his voice. "There is a lot of talk about what's going on in the Federation. We can't afford to miss this."

Kell decided the best approach was the truth. "I would rather stay on board."

Benitez looked at him seriously and said, "Hmmm." Then he smiled and shook his head. "Not an option. You have to come with me."

"I refuse," Kell said in a tone that would brook no argument...from anyone other than Benitez.

"Look, Flash, I heard about what happened between you and Parrish."

The Klingon was astonished that this might be true. What had happened and then ended between himself and Ensign Parrish was not a subject that would be of interest to warriors.

These are humans, not *warriors,* he reminded himself.

"And no matter how much you want to, you can't sit in your quarters and mope," he said.

Kell's blood stirred. He knew what the human slang word "mope" meant. Not only did it not apply to him, it was impossible, *no, unthinkable,* for a Klingon. Of course, he could explain none of that to the human, even if Benitez could understand.

"I have seen starbases before," the Klingon said. Strictly speaking, that was true. He had spent a few days on a starbase before he was posted to the *Enterprise.* Yet he had made a point to venture out of his quarters as little as possible to minimize his risk of exposure.

"And it may be a long time before you see one again," Benitez countered. "I can't let you miss this."

"You cannot force me," Kell said.

"You are serious about this?" Benitez said.

Finally, the human sees the obvious, Kell thought.

Then Benitez did something that surprised the Klingon: He sat on the nearest of the two beds. Concern ran over the human's face.

"I didn't know it was that bad," Benitez said.

The Klingon did not know where this was going, but he was immediately on his guard.

"Do you want to talk about it?" the human asked.

"No," the Klingon replied.

Benitez seemed to have come to a decision. "Fine, stay, but I can't let you stay alone. I will be right here, if you want to talk."

The Klingon watched in horror as Benitez leaned back on the bed, making himself comfortable.

"Flash, you're not going to regret this," Benitez said as they headed down the corridor.

When they reached the transporter room, the rest of their squad was there, except for their squad leader, Sam Fuller. The new squad was made up of the survivors of the System 1324 incident.

Ensign Jawer looked well. His burned hands were still pink and had a light bandage wrapped around each palm. Ensign Clark was no longer wearing her sling and seemed to be completely healed.

Leslie Parrish looked…well. She gave Benitez and Kell a polite smile and said, casually, "It will be a minute; Chief Brantley is swearing in a new squad of recruits."

For a moment, no one spoke. They all knew that the officers inside were replacing one of the two squads lost on the last mission.

Parrish's expression gave no indication that their last exchange had been...strained. *Perhaps she has forgotten it already,* Kell thought. He didn't see how that was possible. His own blood was burning and roaring in his ears at the sight of her.

Yet she turned away and resumed a conversation with her new partner, Ensign Sobel, who had been part of Chief Brantley's squad when the battle against the Orions had begun.

A moment later, Captain Kirk and Lieutenant Commander Giotto exited the transporter room. The captain nodded to the assembled squad and said, "Ensigns."

Then Chief Brantley came out with six new security officers. To Kell's eyes, they looked impossibly soft and innocent. Looking around at his own squad, he saw warriors who had been tested in battle, who had prevailed against a foe that should have overwhelmed them.

Did the recruits who just left have the same courage, the same strength in their blood? He could not believe that it was possible, yet he had seen humans do the impossible—over and over.

What did that mean for the coming Klingon attack? Would the humans give the Klingon Defense Force a surprise?

Not if he and the other Infiltrators who were spread throughout the Federation and Starfleet did their jobs well.

When he had been training for this mission, he had asked one of his superiors why Klingons had to hide their true faces to defeat the Earthers. If the Empire was truly more powerful—which no Klingon would dispute—why not face the Earthers directly?

The response then had been that the Earthers' own tendency toward deceit and treachery meant that the Klingons would have to adopt some of the enemy's methods to win the coming battle. Ultimately, his instructor had reminded him of the Klingon proverb "The victor is always right."

At the time, the Klingon had accepted the explanation. He had heard many tales of Earther treachery during his training, as he had heard many tales of the vile Captain Kirk. He had reasoned that the Empire might even be able to teach the Earthers something of honor when the Federation was part of the Empire.

Now Kell held none of his previous illusions. He had seen honor among humans. He had learned the truth about Captain Kirk, who was both honorable and brave, and now held Kell in an honor debt.

Kell now questioned whether the Empire had the strength to defeat the Federation in open battle, or even if such a course was wise or honorable. Kahless taught, "It is better to have strong friends than strong enemies."

In his blood, he sensed that humans could make very powerful allies of the Empire and would make very poor subjects.

While he knew he would do his duty, he was glad he would not have to do it today.

Suddenly, Kell was glad that Benitez had pressured him to come to the starbase. He had fought with these people and he knew with certainty that they were the last friends he would have on this side of the River of Blood.

They entered the transporter room together and a moment later appeared on a transporter pad on the starbase. Outside the transporter room, they entered a wide and long corridor that had a large number of Starfleet and civilian personnel going back and forth.

Predictably, Benitez spoke first. "Okay, where to?"

What followed was what seemed like an endless discussion of the possibilities for recreation and shopping. Most of the group, including Kell himself, wanted to get a drink.

"If you want to find ale, go to a bar," he said.

The rest of the group was silent for a moment.

"That's what I like about you, Flash," Benitez said. "You don't say much but when you do you get right to the heart of the matter."

"There's the Starfleet canteen," Ensign Clark suggested.

Ensign Sobel spoke up. "Apparently, there's a great place in the civilian sector."

Clark shook her head. "According to the liberty guidelines, we are supposed to—"

"The key word there is *guidelines*," Benitez interjected. "And guidelines are not regulations."

"It is decided," the Klingon said.

"Lead on," Benitez said to Ensign Sobel.

Twenty minutes later they approached a nondescript door with a sign above it in an alien script that Kell did not recognize.

"It's Vulcan," Benitez offered. "It means 'party.' "

"A Vulcan bar?" Kell asked.

"It's not run by Vulcans. I think the name is supposed to be a joke," Sobel said, stepping forward.

The doors slid open and revealed something that the Klingon did not think could exist within the flat gray institutional construction of the starbase.

It was impossible to tell the color of the walls, because it was simply too dark. There was a long bar on one wall, with tables strewn haphazardly around the center. The far wall was a huge window overlooking space.

A large human civilian stopped the group with a raised hand. A short animated conversation erupted between Ensign Sobel and the human. Then the man lowered his hand and they were allowed to pass.

The group made their way to the bar.

Inside, the Klingon could see some of the patrons. They were a motley collection of races. He saw civilian Andorians, Tellarites, and a number of others he did not recognize.

"This is what the Federation is all about," Ensign Sobel said.

"Drunken rabble?" the Klingon replied.

Sobel smiled. "You see drunken rabble and I see many different people and cultures coming together to form one group of—"

"Drunken rabble," Benitez offered, breaking out into laughter.

It was early in the day, so they were able to find enough open space at the bar for all of them.

Before they reached the bar, he heard Jawer's voice call out, "Now, there is a beautiful sight."

Everyone turned to see what he was looking at, and the Klingon saw the *Enterprise* hanging in space. The Klingon had to admit that the lines of the ship were graceful and it had a compelling long-legged beauty. He also knew that warriors in the Klingon Defense Force derided the design, but Kell knew that the vessel contained strength that would surprise any Klingon battle cruiser that faced it.

At the bar, Ensign Sobel announced, "The first round is on me. How does Romulan ale sound?"

Ensign Clark frowned. "That is not only against liberty guidelines, it is against Starfleet regulations *and* illegal."

"Do you want one?" Sobel asked.

"Only if it's aged," Clark replied seriously.

Nodding, Ensign Sobel began speaking to the bartender, a male Trill. The conversation was loud and animated.

The Klingon took the time to survey the bar. Reflexively he noted the most dangerous species and mentally reviewed the best fighting techniques to use against each. It was then he noticed that there were very few humans in the bar, and his squad was the only one wearing Starfleet uniforms.

Turning back to the bar, Kell saw that Sobel and the bartender were still…negotiating. Then he saw a Klingon trader approach the bar. In his surprise, he could not help staring, suddenly sure that the fellow Klingon would recognize and expose him.

Turning away before the Klingon caught his stare and answered the challenge he would have seen in it, Kell focused on Benitez. But his roommate was turning toward the Klingon. Then the human did something that shocked Kell.

In clear Klingon, Benitez looked directly at the trader and said, "nutlhej SuvwI'"—or, in English, "A warrior is among us."

For a moment, Kell was certain that Benitez was an Infiltrator, like Kell himself.

The Klingon trader was automatically alert and shouted, "nuq DaneH?" Or "What do you want?" in English. As he spoke, the Klingon leaned closer to Benitez, who responded in heavily accented Klingon with, "ngem lopwI' vIrI'." Or, in English, "I greet a forest reveler."

Then Kell understood. Benitez was no Infiltrator; he was merely a human with a bit of Klingon language and terrible pronunciation.

Though Kell was relieved, the Klingon was suddenly enraged and reached out with both hands to push Benitez toward the bar. The human was caught by surprise and then had his back pressed to the bar.

"Hey, hey," Benitez protested. "I was just saying hello."

Clearly, Benitez did not know how much danger he was in, but Kell did, and he acted immediately.

Grabbing the Klingon by the shoulder, he executed a move that was more than a push but less than a throw. Pulling the trader to him, he pushed out with his hip and stepped forward. The result was that the Klingon was forced off Benitez and Kell was now between them.

The Klingon trader's face betrayed his own surprise. Yet, he was able to strike a clumsy blow in Kell's direction. Kell deflected the blow easily but restrained himself from striking back, yet. A full-scale brawl would present too many dangers to his mission. There were too many ways for him to be exposed.

"Stop!" Kell shouted to the Klingon.

The trader responded with a string of Klingon expletives, and another blow.

Kell blocked the blow and gave the Klingon a hard shove backward. He realized at once that the Klingon was untrained. He would be depressingly easy to best, and Kell realized that he could have taken the trader when he was a child.

"wa' luHIv jav 'e' lumaS tera' nuchpu' net Sov"— "Six against one, typical cowardly Earther odds," the trader said in Klingon, and Kell realized two things simultaneously. The Klingon spoke no English, and silence had descended on this part of the bar. All eyes in the area were watching the two men.

"jImob. veQ SoH. ngeDqu' HeghlIj. quvbe'pu' yInlIj; lI'be'," he shouted in perfect Klingon. Or, in English, "I need no help to take your honorless, worthless life."

The Klingon was plainly shocked to hear his language spoken so forcefully by a human. Again he recovered quickly. This time, he threw his whole body at Kell, who sidestepped the blow, grabbing the Klingon by the scruff of the neck and guiding his head straight into the bar.

The trader hit with a resounding—and satisfying—crack. Kell maintained his hold on the traders clothing and lifted the Klingon's dazed head.

"choqaDqa'chugh vaj bIHegh," he shouted. "Test me again, and die!"

Kell knew the trader would trouble them no more, yet he could not resist humiliating this insult to Klingon blood. Reaching out, he brought the back of his hand across the trader's face.

It was a deadly insult, but the Klingon trader did not seem prepared to die to answer it.

Later, Kell would realize that the humiliation was unwise given the consequences. Yet, even if he had known what would follow, he would not have been able to resist.

Releasing the Klingon, Kell watched his eyes burn. But the trader turned and walked away. Following him with his eyes, Kell did not turn around until the Klingon was on the far side of the bar, near a group of Nausicaans.

When Kell did turn to the rest of his squad, they were looking at him with respect. He thought Leslie was looking at him as well, but she quickly turned away, resuming her conversation with Ensign Sobel.

"Thanks, Flash," Benitez said. "That's one I owe you. Well, another one anyway."

"It was my pleasure," Kell said.

"I could have handled him, you know," Benitez said.

Kell thought about it. Starfleet did teach basic self-defense. And the Klingon had been teaching some rudimentary *Mok'bara* techniques to the squad at Chief Fuller's request. Benitez might well have surprised the Klingon trader.

The Klingon nodded and saw that the bartender had finally produced a bottle of Romulan ale and was pouring it into six glasses.

Ensign Sobel raised his glass first and said, "Here is to greater understanding and peace among the galaxy's different people, even cranky Klingons."

The others lifted their glasses. Then he saw they were looking at him and he raised his own glass.

There was only one way to drink Romulan ale and that was quickly—dallying risked injury. He finished his in a single fast swallow.

The burning only lasted a moment and slowly faded into pleasant warmth. For a moment, his raging thoughts quieted. Then he saw Parrish leaning close to Ensign Sobel.

"I didn't know you spoke Klingon, Flash. Any more surprises in you?" Benitez asked.

Kell was immediately on his guard, but he saw that Benitez was sincere in his question.

"I learned it when I was young, from a group of Klingons on my world," Kell said.

"You speak it very well," Benitez said.

"And you speak it terribly," the Klingon countered.

Benitez smiled. "I understand it better. I know my accent is terrible and I could never master all the spitting and shouting it requires. I studied for a little while at the Klingon Language Institute when I was in high school. It was for a galactic citizenship merit badge in the Starfleet Scouts."

But the Klingon barely heard him. His mind was already elsewhere as he saw Parrish lean forward and laugh at something Ensign Sobel said.

Chapter Six

KAREL ENTERED the second officer's quarters. Klak was standing, waiting for him. It was a sign of respect, a sign that the Klingon took him seriously.

"Senior weapons officer," Klak said, nodding and gesturing to a seat next to the wall. In front of that seat was a table and on that table was a large bowl of squirming *gagh*.

The second officer took his breakfast live, Karel noted, as he did himself. He sat and watched as the second officer took the seat opposite him.

"Eat," Klak said, grabbing a handful of worms.

Karel did. The *gagh* was good and neither Klingon spoke until the worms were gone.

"You have done well, Senior Weapons Officer," Klak said.

It was true, Karel knew, but it was unusual for a

Klingon officer to offer praise so casually. Karel was immediately on his guard.

"I am pleased that you have made the most of the opportunity I gave you. The efficiency of your disruptor room has improved a great deal," Klak said.

Again true, but Karel noted that the second officer had pointed out his own role in Karel's success.

"I think you may go far on this ship, and in the Klingon Defense Force," Klak said.

"I serve the Empire," Karel said flatly.

Klak dismissed that with a wave. "We all serve the Empire, but we also serve ourselves. What are your ambitions?"

"To crush the Empire's enemies," Karel said.

Klak smiled and Karel noted that the smile was not pleasant, even by Klingon standards. "Earthers," he said. "You would be better able to crush them on the bridge, as the weapons commander."

Raising an eyebrow, Karel said, "The ship has a capable weapons commander, Commander Koloth," Karel said.

"True, but we are talking about the future," Klak said. "And if you are a better officer, then your duty demands that you challenge and replace Koloth."

"When I am ready, I will do my duty," Karel said. "Until then, I have much to learn."

Klak smiled again and said, "I told you I might call on your loyalty, Karel."

"Yes," Karel said.

"Now I ask you to take an additional duty. I need to add to my personal guards," Klak said.

Karel was genuinely surprised. "Surely there are others—"

"I have seen you fight. You bested Gash, who was much bigger than you, and then another one in the same day. You fight with the blood of a warrior," Klak said.

"My disruptor room..." Karel said.

"You will keep your command, but from time to time I will ask you to...assist me on off-duty periods."

Karel's blood called out a warning, but he could not refuse Klak. The second officer had shown him respect and could have ordered him without asking. "I go where I am needed," Karel said.

"Good. It will mean additional duty, but you will get some experience on the bridge. An ambitious warrior could learn much," Klak said.

As Karel left the second officer's quarters, his blood continued its warning. Everything Klak had said had made sense, yet he was convinced that there was something else at work here. He felt sure that Klak had not lied to him—at least not exactly—but the second officer had failed to mention his true intentions, whatever those were.

Karel decided not to worry about it. For the moment, he would do his duty and stay on his guard.

"What is it, Spock?" Kirk said, walking into the sensor control room with Dr. McCoy in tow.

"I have tied the *Enterprise*'s sensors into the starbase sensor array. The combined system has allowed us extremely long range," Spock said.

"You've found something?" Kirk asked.

"Yes," the Vulcan said. "By carefully calibrating sensors I was able to search for specific irregularities in warp reactors. These irregularities form a distinctive power signature, allowing sensors to scan for specific warp-field technology."

"Blast it, Spock, what have you found, in English please?" McCoy said.

"Orions, Doctor. By scanning for Orion technology, I was able to plot dozens of warp systems using Orion equipment in this sector," Spock said.

"Interesting, Spock," Kirk said, "but we can't chase down every Orion ship in the sector. There are too many Orion vessels operating legitimately, or at least operating without a connection to the alert."

"Yes, but there was one signature that stood out. It is being generated by an extremely large warp reactor," Spock said.

"How large?" Kirk asked.

"Several orders of magnitude larger than the warp reactor that powers this ship," Spock said.

"What possible use...?" McCoy said.

"Only one, Doctor. Deep-core mining. Rapid, deep-core mining," Spock said. "This would be of concern by itself. Deep-core mining operations are extremely destructive to planetary environments. They are illegal on Federation worlds that support life. However, there is something that makes this situation even more troubling."

Spock hit one of his controls and a star map appeared on one of the screens above his station. The target system was outlined in red.

Kirk saw the problem immediately. "Spock, that is very close to Klingon space."

"Practically in the Klingons' backyard," McCoy added.

"Precisely, Doctor," the Vulcan said.

"Spock, what is deep-core mining used for?" Kirk asked.

"Very expensive and rapid mining operations like this one, particularly illegal operations, which must be set up and concluded quickly to avoid detection are only practical for extraction of extremely valuable materials," the Vulcan said.

"Dilithium crystals," Kirk said. "They are mining for dilithium crystals."

"Undoubtedly," Spock said. "If the Klingon Empire is indeed planning a major offensive to launch in the next several months, they will need a large supply of starship-grade crystals."

"How long has the mine been active?" Kirk said.

"By reviewing sensor records, I deduce that it has not been active for long enough to yield many crystals so far," Spock said.

"Then it is not too late to stop them before the Klingons get their hands on a *large supply of starship-grade crystals*," Kirk said.

"Most likely, Captain, but there is another reason the mine has to be shut down immediately," Spock said. "The planet has an indigenous, humanoid population. It is a pretechnology society about which we know very little. The people were discovered by a remote probe. Estimates are of a planetary population of approximately one hundred thousand beings."

"Who won't be there for much longer if the core mining runs its course," Kirk said. "Mr. Spock, we need to get under way as soon as possible. Please start recalling the crew from liberty on the starbase." The captain regretted doing it. Opportunities for recreation off the ship might be few and far between given the current alert. Even more unsettling was the fact that most of the crew did not yet know about the danger the Federation was facing. But none of that could be helped now. The crew would do its duty. For now, there was a planet full of sentient beings threatened by an illegal operation.

"What is the status of our resupply?" Kirk asked.

"Essential supplies and equipment have already been brought on board. We can accelerate the schedule immediately and then even more as more crew return to the ship," the Vulcan replied.

"How long before we can get under way?" Kirk asked.

"Four hours, thirty-seven minutes," the science officer said, without checking the computer terminal in front of him, or even blinking for that matter.

"Thank you, Mr. Spock. I had better warn Scotty that we'll be leaving," Kirk said, heading for the door.

It seems she forms attachments very quickly, the Klingon thought, watching Leslie Parrish talking with Ensign Sobel.

"Flash, if I am not mistaken, you were the one who ended it with her," Benitez said from his position next to him.

The Klingon suddenly realized that he had spoken the thought out loud. He took a moment to curse the ale and the Romulans who created it. Then he scowled at his roommate.

He sensed someone appear next to him. Turning, he saw green skin. Orion, his mind screamed. Immediately, he was alert and reaching for his phaser.

By the time his hand was at his side, he realized two

things simultaneously. First, his phaser was not there, because sidearms were not allowed on the starbase for off-duty personnel. Second, the Orion next to him was not a threat. The Orion next to him was female—very female.

She smiled at him and he noticed that she was wearing next to nothing and wearing it very well.

She smelled good, he realized, wonderful even. He found that he could not take his eyes from her. She simply ordered a drink and smiled at him.

She smiled at him. Even her smile was intoxicating. As intoxicating as Romulan ale, but much more pleasant.

He realized his blood was burning.

The pheromones, he realized. It was her pheromones.

By force of will, he turned away from her, looking to his right. He saw Benitez and beyond him Leslie Parrish, who for the first time all evening was looking directly at him.

She scowled and turned away.

By now, Ensign Sobel was staring at the Orion female, as was Jawer, and as was Benitez.

The Klingon noted that she had not attracted as much attention among the other male patrons nearby. Presumably, the different alien species were less susceptible to her scent...and other charms. Kell felt his eyes drawn back to her and sensed the other males in his squad hovering over his shoulder. They were leaning into each other and pressing against him to be closer to her.

Kell felt a rough shove against his shoulder.

He looked up. And up.

Towering above him was a very large Nausicaan. He thought the alien might be sneering at him. With Nausicaans it was hard to tell. Their faces seemed to be frozen in perpetual sneers.

For the moment, Kell ignored the Nausicaan and followed the female with his eyes. She turned once, smiled at him again, and continued walking toward the window on the far wall.

"Earther," someone bellowed in his ear. That shocked him out of his reverie. He turned to see the Nausicaan *sneering* at him. It was the second time that day that someone had called him an Earther.

The first one was the Klingon trader. Looking past the Nausicaan, Kell saw a group of Nausicaans—eight of them. He also saw the Klingon trader who was looking at him and working up a sneer of his own.

Suddenly, Kell was sure the Klingon trader had set whatever was about to happen up with the Nausicaans. He was equally certain that whatever was about to happen was going to be very bad.

"You bothering my female, *Earther?*" the Nausicaan said, prodding Kell with a finger.

He said "Earther" with a particularly nasty sneer. The Klingon knew that the term was a great insult among Nausicaans, as it was among Klingons.

"Did you hear me, Earther?" the Nausicaan said.

Kell did not bother to respond. He knew from experience that Nausicaans initiated a verbal exchange before they began an attack. They used the escalating war of words to work up their own courage and then struck.

Kell, however, had no patience for such childish games. He believed the Klingon axiom *The best attack is a direct attack.*

Slowly, he rose from his bar stool. He quickly calculated his best chance for victory. If he incapacitated their leader quickly, the other Nausicaans might decide not to get involved.

On the other hand, they would still see odds of eight Nausicaans against six humans and would probably try to finish them. Still, eight Nausicaans were better than nine.

He knew the humans would fight beside him. And they would fight well. He hoped that would be enough.

When he was on his feet, Kell noted that the Nausicaan was a full head taller than he was. The alien would be a challenge that the Klingon would enjoy.

"Are you deaf as well as stupid, Earther?" the Nausicaan said, turning to his friends and laughing.

Rearing back, Kell prepared to make his move. He would have to come out on the other side of the Nausicaan. With his back to the bar, Kell would not have the room to maneuver. In close quarters the Nausicaan would use his size and strength to great advantage.

The Klingon knew he could not fight his adversaries' fight, not if he wanted to walk away from this bar in one piece.

Before he could execute his move, a slim figure interposed itself between Kell and the Nausicaan. Checking his own movement just in time, Kell watched as Benitez put up his hand and said, "Hey, none of us wants trouble."

The Nausicaan laughed. "Maybe I want trouble," he said.

That was it, the pretense was gone. The battle would follow very quickly now.

It came even quicker than he anticipated. The Nausicaan reared back with his left hand, feinted with it, and struck quickly with his right fist—which, Kell noted, was the size of a medium-sized *targ*.

Benitez moved with astonishing speed. Rather than try to block the blow, he leaned into the Nausicaan and ducked. He came out beside and slightly behind the alien. In nearly one fluid motion, Benitez brought his foot in front of his opponent and pushed him forward into the bar.

Carried forward by the push and the momentum of his own blow, the Nausicaan crashed into the bar. It was a variation on the move Kell had used on the Klingon trader to great effect.

This time, however, the Nausicaan was not nearly incapacitated by a blow to the head. Instead, he hit the bar with his stomach and turned around, looking truly angry.

"Like I said," Benitez said, "we do not want any trouble, but we are pretty good at dealing with it."

By his tone, Kell could see that Benitez seemed to think that the confrontation might be over. There was something noble in his naïveté, but it was a mistake few beings ever had a chance to make twice with an angry Nausicaan.

The Nausicaan lifted one hand slowly in a gesture of appeasement. Benitez gave a smile that told Kell the human once again didn't realize the danger he was in.

Kell did, and he saw the blade immediately.

The hand that the Nausicaan had kept low was moving and holding a knife. It was smaller than a *d'k tahg,* about the size of a Klingon assassin's knife.

Reacting quickly and without thinking, Kell raised his right hand and brought it down, hard, on the Nausicaan's knife hand.

It was only when he made contact with the alien's wrist that the Klingon realized he was still holding his heavy glass mug. The glass hit the Nausicaan's wrist with a satisfying snap and Kell was confident that the wrist was broken.

Kell immediately looked for and found the knife on the ground. He kicked it under the bar and out of reach. The Nausicaan was leaning over, cradling his wrist, but the Klingon did not want to underestimate the alien.

The Klingon had to suppress his instinct to simply kill the Nausicaan now. It was the wisest course, given what he knew of Nausicaans, but it was not what a human Starfleet officer would do. And for now, he still had to play that role.

Grabbing him by the shoulder, the Klingon shoved the Nausicaan leader aside and to the ground.

This all took seconds, but it was long enough for the rest of the bar to take notice. The immediate area had gone quiet and some patrons had begun moving their tables toward the window.

The result was that there was a semicircle of open space around the eight Nausicaans and the six Starfleet officers. Looking over his left shoulder, Kell saw that all six members of his squad were lined up next to him. With pride, he noted that they had remembered some of their *Mok'bara* training and had stepped away from the bar two steps to give themselves maneuvering room.

The Nausicaan leader got up slowly, still cradling his injured wrist. He made his way back to his comrades.

Kell considered the other Nausicaans, who were standing in a confused jumble, unlike the neat line of readiness that Kell's security squad formed.

Their leader had instigated the fight and had been clearly and soundly beaten. If they were an honorable people, they would simply accept the defeat and leave the bar.

But the Nausicaans were clearly not an honorable people.

Their leader joined their ranks, glared at the Starfleet people, and shouted something in the Nausicaan language.

The aliens talked among themselves. They did not act immediately. Untrained and undisciplined, they needed to work up their courage. They would be sloppy fighters and would not fight as one, as he had no doubt the security squad would do.

Yet the Nausicaans were bigger and stronger. There were also more of them, and any or all of the Nausicaans might have blades.

As Starfleet officers, the humans would wait until the attackers struck before they fought back. It was a human principle and their strict adherence to it was admirable.

But he had seen too many humans die nobly as they followed their principles. They could not afford to wait. "Watch for blades!" he shouted to his friends as he launched himself into the center of the Nausicaans, aiming a combination of blows at the largest ones.

As humans, the Starfleet officers would not strike the Nausicaans first, but Kell knew they would quickly come to his aid. His ears and peripheral vision told him this was already happening.

For the moment, he could not concern himself with their welfare. He was focused on the Nausicaan in front of him. The alien he had hit first was on his knees, trying to shake off his disorientation. The Klingon did not wait for that to happen. He brought up his own knee into the Nausicaan's face, catching the alien in the forehead.

The Nausicaan fell backward with a dull thud.

By then, the two Nausicaans on either side of the Klingon had begun to act. The one on Kell's right grabbed his arm, while the other pushed him to keep him off balance.

He saw a flash of metal, and before he realized what the Nausicaan on his left was doing, a female voice he recognized yelled out, "Knife!"

An instant later, a body hurled itself at the knife-wielding Nausicaan. Before the Klingon raised his forearm to deflect the knife, a blur in Starfleet red crashed into the Nausicaan's arm, forcing the arm into an outward arc.

This was unfortunate for the Nausicaan who was standing next to him. He took the point of the knife straight in his thigh. He let out a howl and grabbed the Nausicaan who stabbed him. The aliens grappled each other and went down to the ground in a mass of shouts and limbs.

Kell took in the confusing tangle of Starfleet red and Nausicaans as they tussled in the ten meters or so around him. Then suddenly the Nausicaan whose wrist Kell had broken reappeared suddenly. He was standing behind Leslie Parrish. He grabbed a chair with his good hand and began raising it over her head.

With her back turned, Parrish didn't see the danger. In fact, she was looking at him, asking him something.

Once again, Kell acted without thinking. He charged, throwing his weight into the alien. As soon as he made contact with the Nausicaan's midsection, he grabbed the broken wrist and twisted it as hard as he could.

He felt the weight of the chair momentarily on his back. At first he thought he had been hit, but then he realized that the Nausicaan had simply dropped the chair on him.

From his position on the ground, the Nausicaan reached out with his good hand, hitting Kell in the side with a glancing blow.

Kell decided he already had had too much trouble from this one. The Klingon grabbed the Nausicaan's good arm with both hands and brought it down as hard as he could on his knee. The snap of bone was surprisingly loud given the noise in the bar.

For the first time, Kell was able to take a second to survey his surroundings. Two Nausicaans were still fighting over the knife, while one was bleeding from a wound to his thigh.

Then he quickly scanned for red tunics and saw that all of his squad was accounted for and in good condition. In fact, they seemed to be thriving.

Kell saw Benitez let loose with a very strong combination of strikes that forced a larger Nausicaan against the bar. The Nausicaan was fighting back, but Benitez was able to deflect the blows easily with some standard Starfleet blocks.

Interesting, Kell thought, Benitez had combined the *Mok'bara* strikes Kell had taught the squad with human defensive techniques. As a Klingon style of fighting, *Mok'bara* relied heavily on powerful strikes, with less attention paid to defensive maneuvers. But humans valued life highly, even their own, and took great pains to preserve it. That came out even in their fighting.

Less than two meters away, Ensign Sobel had somehow gotten a Nausicaan onto the bar and was pushing him over the other side.

Ensign Clark threw one of the aliens over his shoulder. He landed flat on his back—and stayed down.

Kell noted that few of the bar's patrons had taken much interest in the fight, except to keep their distance.

Together, he and Parrish watched the Nausicaan leader struggle to his feet. The task was made more difficult because he was trying not to touch the ground with either of his injured arms.

The large alien finally stood up and gave Kell and Parrish a contemptuous look.

"Go ahead, make a move, *please!*" Parrish said.

The Nausicaan decided not to and simply backed away.

Then the blast of energy-weapon fire cut through the din of the waning battle.

Chapter Seven

"I HAVE THE... *Endeavor,* I think, sir," Science Officer Okuda said.

"On screen," Captain Rodriguez ordered.

The image on the main viewscreen shifted from the view of the open space to a close-up of a ship. No not a ship. At least not a whole one.

Lieutenant Justman felt his mouth hang open as he saw the primary hull of the *Endeavor* hanging in space before them.

The secondary hull and the warp nacelles were... gone.

Their captain must have separated the primary hull before the warp-core breach, Justman realized. The battle must have been intense and the damage very bad.

The magnification increased on the screen and Justman could see that the primary hull had been damaged in the fighting. The saucer-shaped hull was scarred and pitted. And in at least three places he could see significant hull breaches.

The damage was terrible, but the primary hull was basically intact and that meant one thing. A single thought, a single word flashed onto Justman's mind. Without realizing it, he spoke the thought aloud.

"Survivors," he said.

"Exactly, and they are our first priority," Captain Rodriguez said. "Klingon cruisers?" he asked.

"Holding their position," Justman said, taking a look at his tactical readout.

The Klingons were sizing them up, Justman felt certain.

That would give them some time. Perhaps just seconds, but enough time for the captain to do something—enough time to give the Klingons a surprise.

"What do scanners show, Mr. Okuda?" Rodriguez asked.

"I'm reading at least one hundred human life signs," Okuda replied. "And about twenty nonhuman."

"Klingons?" the captain asked.

Okuda checked his viewer and said, "Yes, sir."

"They've been boarded," Rodriguez said, watching the screen carefully.

"Sir," Okuda said excitedly. "I'm not sure the Klingons have complete control though. I'm showing power spikes. I think it's weapons fire."

Justman felt a wave of hope. Even with their ship crippled, the crew of the *Endeavor* was fighting. Well, the *Yorkshire* was at one hundred percent and he could see the determination on the captain's face. He decided he would not want to be the Klingons right now.

"I have one of the Klingon commanders," the communications officer announced.

"On screen," the captain said, standing.

A moment later a Klingon face dominated the viewscreen. Justman had never seen a Klingon in person and this was the first time he had seen one in a live transmission. The Klingon had a mustache and a short beard. His expression was one of fierce contempt.

"*Earther* commander," the Klingon said. "I am Commander Maarcs, you will—"

"This is Captain Rodriguez of the *United Space Ship Yorkshire*. You will stand down immediately!" the captain shouted. "You are in violation of treaty. Your aggression here is an act of war. You will retrieve the Klingons currently on board the *Endeavor* and return to Klingon space immediately or face destruction."

The Klingon grinned.

It was not a pleasant sight, Justman decided.

"I claim this system in the name of the Klingon Empire. Surrender your ship and I will grant you and your crew quick deaths," Maarcs said.

"Commander Maarcs," Rodriguez said, "you are in no position to make demands. There are two Starfleet ships on their way to this system right now. Withdraw or face the consequences."

The Klingon laughed. "*Earther* Captain," the Klingon said, and the emphasis he placed on the word "Earther" told Justman that it did not have good connotations among Klingons. "There are two Klingon battle cruisers in front of you. And our scanners show that your pathetic ships will arrive about one of your hours after two more Klingon vessels arrive. Surrender now."

"Surrender, to you?" the captain said. "You do not even have control over the *Endeavor*. Even now your pathetic warriors are getting rousted."

That stung the Klingon commander, who could not hide it. Recovering, he said, "We will have the cowardly humans under control soon enough."

"Let me speak to Captain Shannon," Rodriguez said.

The Klingon's face twitched. That told Justman that something was wrong. Perhaps the Klingon did not have Captain Shannon *under control* at the moment.

"No," the Klingon said. "But I offer a gesture to show that I am serious. Watch the *Endeavor*."

The image of the Klingon cut out and was replaced by the close view of the *Endeavor*'s hull.

"Mr. Justman, what do you have on the Klingons?" the Captain said.

Justman took a last look at his data, "Sir, both ships are damaged. I'm showing weak spots in their shields. The *Endeavor* hit them pretty hard before..." The lieutenant commander found he could not finish the sentence. "It looks like they have also suffered some extensive radiation damage. Must have happened when the *Endeavor*'s warp core exploded."

The captain nodded, taking this all in.

"I'm getting weapons locks on the weakest areas of the two ships," Justman concluded.

The captain was about to speak when he was interrupted by Science Officer Okuda, who said, "Sir, there is some activity in the forward airlock. I'm showing a concentration of life signs."

All eyes went to the viewscreen, which showed the top of the *Endeavor*'s primary hull.

"Helm, bring us about," the captain said. "Let's see what's going on."

Justman felt the ship start to move and the view changed to the underside of the *Endeavor*'s hull. He could see the forward airlock clearly.

The door was open, but he could see people in Starfleet uniforms inside, which meant the forcefield was on, holding in the atmosphere.

Then, in a flash of insight, Justman knew what was about to happen. Before the thought had fully formed in his mind, he watched it play out.

The view was close enough that Justman could see the faces of the *Endeavor*'s crew in front. They were frightened but not panicked.

Then there was a shimmer as the airlock's forcefield turned off. The people inside were violently lifted from the deck and propelled with great speed into the void of space.

At the sound of weapons fire, Kell was instantly alert. A blade was one thing. As long as its point didn't find the heart or brain, the medical facilities on board the starbase could repair nearly any injury his squadmates suffered.

An energy weapon was another matter. Even human medical science—which was more highly developed than Klingon medicine—could do nothing to revive someone who had been disintegrated.

Instinctively, he took a single step in front of Ensign Parrish.

Then the red light of another blast lit up the dimly lit bar, which was suddenly completely silent. Searching quickly for the source of the weapons discharges, Kell saw a squad of six armed starbase security officers led by a very angry-looking woman wearing lieutenant braids on the cuffs of her uniform.

The Klingon felt himself relax.

Immediately, the various combatants moved away from one another. The rest of his squad looked relieved, but Kell thought that it was the Nausicaans who were the most fortunate that the authorities had arrived.

The Nausicaans were uncharacteristically docile as the security officer herded them into a group. When they were all together, the leader began to speak, voicing a protest.

"Quiet!" the lieutenant shouted, raising her phaser.

The Nausicaan was immediately silent. The lieutenant barked orders to her squad and four of them escorted the eight Nausicaans out of the bar.

Then, with the two remaining officers flanking her, the lieutenant approached Kell and his squad, who out of habit had fallen into line.

She gave the officers a tight smile and said, "I'm Lieutenant Block. I will be your jailer for today."

Benitez smiled and said, "Our what?"

"Your jailer. You are under arrest for violation of Starfleet regulation one forty-four eight, section five," Block said.

"Arrest, you can't be serious," Benitez said. "They attacked us. It was self-defense."

Lieutenant Block nodded her head in sympathy and Kell felt certain that she would release them. "That's an interesting story, I look forward to hearing the rest of it when you troublemakers are in the brig."

* * *

"See, we were provoked," Benitez said, from his position behind the forcefield of the brig, where the squad was now detained. "In fact, it was remarkable that we were able to neutralize the Nausicaans' threat. Civilians could have been hurt. If it weren't for Flash here—"

"Who?" Lieutenant Block said.

"Ensign Anderson," Benitez said, pointing to Kell. "He disarmed the Nausicaan leader. And then Ensign Parrish disarmed another one. The arms represented a serious threat to the nearby civilians."

"I find that hard to believe, Ensign, since I currently have two injured Nausicaans in the infirmary. They say you initiated an unprovoked attack and ignored their pleas to be left alone."

"There were dozens of witnesses," Ensign Jawer said.

"I have dozens of witnesses who swear they didn't see a thing," she countered.

"You don't believe that," Jawer said.

"What I know for certain is that you six Starfleet officers intentionally ignored liberty guidelines," she said.

"But, the—" Benitez began, but the lieutenant silenced him with a glance.

"Guidelines which are there for your safety," she said.

One of her officers handed Block a data padd, which she scanned quickly.

"I see that I am privileged today," she said, scanning the six people in the brig. "I think you are the most decorated group of officers I have ever had in my brig. Apparently, you have more citations and medals between you than some small crews. Well, after today, you will have something else to add to your permanent Starfleet record."

She glared at the group for a moment; they were all silent. "I would like to make an example of you. Starfleet's mission to seek new races and civilizations is not supposed to include sending them to the nearest hospital. And I am tired of playing den mother to first-year officers who are trying to prove themselves."

Kell shook his head in wonder. Would his mission end right here? Would he spend the balance of the coming war in a Starfleet brig—all because of some Nausicaans were looking for amusement at Starfleet's expense?

"But I am going to release you. It seems the *Enterprise* is needed elsewhere and your commander is convinced you actually make a contribution on board. Captain Kirk pulled some strings with the starbase commander."

Kell and his squad relaxed visibly.

"Do not think you have gotten off easy," she chided them. "I have already spoken to your section chief. He will be arriving shortly to take you back to your ship. From the sound of his voice I have a feeling that by this time tomorrow you will wish you were safely back here in my brig."

As if on cue, the Klingon saw the outer doors open and Sam Fuller come walking into the holding area. He glanced at his squad for a moment and then faced Lieutenant Block.

"I'll take them, Lieutenant," he said.

Block handed Fuller a data padd, which he signed and handed back. On a signal from the lieutenant, one of her men hit a switch and the forcefield disappeared.

"Fall in," Fuller said.

Quickly, Kell's squad formed a line in front of the chief, who walked the line, looking each of the security officers in the eye.

"I am very disappointed in you," he said after a long silence, and Kell felt as if he had disappointed his own father in a matter of honor.

"I have heard Lieutenant Block's report and I know how these things go. This kind of trouble always had a mastermind, a ringleader. I am going to ask you just one question: Who started it?"

The Klingon knew that the answer to that question was simple. It was he who had made a point of humiliating the Klingon trader who had somehow put the Nausicaans up to the fight. From the burning look in Sam Fuller's eyes, he knew that he had something special planned for the ensign responsible.

Kell did not hesitate, he took one step forward... and saw the five people next to him do the same. The Klingon was surprised. While he was actually responsible, the rest of the squad had stepped forward only to spare him additional punishment.

The chief's face, however, registered no surprise.

"I see. Then you will all receive the same punishment," he said. "Let's move. You have taken up enough of Lieutenant Block's time already."

The chief nodded to Block and headed out the door. But as Fuller turned, Kell could have sworn he saw the ghost of a grin pass between Fuller and Block.

Chapter Eight

KELL WALKED INTO the security office and Chief Fuller looked up.

"Sit down, Jon," he said crisply.

The Klingon sat.

"I called you in here to finish our earlier discussion about your future."

"My future?" Kell asked. He had assumed the subject of their discussion would be punishment.

"Your future with Starfleet. Have you decided what you would like to do? I repeat the same offer I made before. You are being offered discharge with full honors. And no one would think less of you for taking it. Your contribution in the incident in System 1324 will be remembered in this service and on this ship whatever you decide."

"I would like to continue my...service, sir," Kell said.

Fuller nodded. "I thought as much. I seem to be able to teach you all everything but sense."

"Have you spoken to the others?" Kell asked.

"Yes, you all seem determined to ignore reason," he said, and Kell heard a distinct note of pride in Fuller's voice.

The chief stood. "Come on, the captain has a special briefing for us," he said.

"What about our...punishment," Kell asked, following Fuller out the door.

"It will have to wait," Sam said as they strode down the corridor.

The two men reached the turbolift and the Klingon watched the chief enter. For an instant, he watched Fuller draw a painful breath as he turned his body inside the lift. Kell followed and looked closely at the chief, who was sweating on his forehead.

Suddenly, the Klingon realized that Fuller was in a significant amount of pain. His wounds obviously had not healed completely and normal movement was taking some effort.

This disturbed the Klingon in a way he could not explain. He had seen the blast that hit Fuller's position inside the caves. Yet even then Kell could not believe that Fuller had been dead. The human seemed indestructible, as if force of will guaranteed his survival.

The Klingon knew such thinking was foolish. Yet in his time with humans he had seen many things that were foolish but also true.

Now he was seeing evidence that Fuller was still injured, reminding him how close the human had come to death.

His reverie was broken when they arrived outside the briefing room. Benitez and Sobel entered just ahead of them; then Fuller and Kell followed.

Captain Kirk and Mr. Spock were inside the briefing room, as well as Security Chief Giotto and Section Chief Brantley.

Once they were assembled, Captain Kirk wasted no time beginning. "I was pleased to hear that all of you choose to stay with Starfleet," the captain said. "I am now going to ask you to accompany me on an important mission to stop the Orions from completing a plan to seriously damage Federation security."

Kell felt a pang of satisfaction. The Orions were dishonorable creatures. Any mission that helped put a stop to one of their cowardly plots would be a mission filled with honor.

Then the Klingon remembered that if he would be accompanying the captain, his duty was to kill this human to whom he owed his life. That had to be his first priority. If he wasted time in seeking satisfaction in killing Orions, he risked dying before he could fulfill his ultimate duty to the Empire.

The Vulcan hit a control on the computer and a star system appeared on the briefing room viewscreen.

"This is System 7348, which is less than ten light-years from Klingon space. Remote probes tell us that it has a thriving indigenous population of sentient, pretechnological humanoids. The planet is threatened by an illegal Orion core-mining operation. We have to put a stop to that operation, before it kills the beings on that planet. I would like you to join me on the landing party to investigate," Kirk said.

Two weeks before, the Klingon would not have believed that the cowardly humans he had learned about in the Empire would ever risk their lives for primitives they did not know. Now he knew that such behavior, odd as it was, was normal for them.

Humans, he had learned, lived by their principles. Captain Kirk, he reckoned, would be willing to die on such a mission. To the best of his ability, Kell vowed to give the captain a good death. He owed at least that much to the man he owed his life.

"Now I am going to share with you highly classified information that I believe pertains directly to this mission." Kirk paused for a moment, studying the security squad in front of him. "The Klingon Empire is planning for war with the Federation."

Kell's squad gasped in surprise at the news. The Klingon did as well, but for a different reason. He could not believe that the humans knew of the Empire's plan when so many Klingons did not.

He noted that chiefs Fuller and Brantley did not react, which told him they already knew.

"This is highly classified information and I am personally authorizing your new clearance to hear it. Starfleet believes the conflict to be inevitable unless the current political climate changes. Further, Command believes the attack will begin seven months from now. Secrecy is important, because the diplomatic corps is still trying to diffuse the situation," Kirk said.

Seven months. So the humans knew things that even I do not, Kell thought. Yet the time frame fit what Kell knew and could guess.

"We now believe," Kirk continued, "that the incident

in System 1324 was part of a Klingon plot to use Orion agents to test Starfleet response and capabilities. We further believe that the Orions' mining operation in System 7348 is there to provide dilithium crystals for the Klingon war effort."

Kell was stunned and was barely able to keep his face composed. *No,* his mind screamed. *It is impossible.*

All Klingons did not all follow Kahless's path to honor, but the Klingon people had their principles, just as the humans did. They did their own fighting. They did not hide behind tricks and subterfuge. Yet even as the thought formed in his mind, the Klingon realized that his presence on the *Enterprise* proved that false.

The Empire had abandoned many of its principles to give him a human's face to fight the Federation from within. If that was possible, anything was possible.

Even as the Klingon searched for ways to refute what Kirk was saying as human deceit, his blood told him that the true deception was much nearer to him.

The captain spoke for a few minutes longer and Kell managed to retain most of what he said.

Then Sam Fuller spoke. "I'm afraid that I will not be able to go with you," he said, which shocked Kell out of his reverie. In its own way, it was as surprising as what Kirk had said.

"I'm afraid that Dr. McCoy has grounded me for another two weeks. Section Chief Brantley will accompany you on this mission," he said. The chief did not look pleased, but Kell was forced to admit that he also did not look well. That notion shook him again.

So much of what he believed had changed since he had come on board the *Enterprise.* He had learned that humans had honor. And he had learned that there was more dishonor in his own Empire than he had ever seen before.

Yet he had found some new things to believe in as he saw Kahless's spirit alive in the unlikely group of humans around him.

Foreboding rose in his blood and a fear for himself that he had never felt before. Kell sensed that he would lose something more valuable than his life on this mission. He was suddenly certain that he would lose his honor, and that it would happen very soon.

While a Klingon warrior did not fear the consequences of a just battle, he knew that this battle was far from just. He found that his only satisfaction came from the fact that Sam Fuller would not see what would transpire on the planet.

A hand reached out and grabbed Karel as he walked along the corridor. His training took over immediately and he barely kept himself from striking Second Officer Klak.

"I have a duty for you," Klak said.

"I am due in my disruptor room," Karel said.

"Not anymore. I have assigned your relief officer to this cycle," the second officer said.

Karel's blood called out a warning. His relief officer was more ambitious than he was capable. He would see an additional shift as a further cementing of his position. Karel had no doubt that the officer would be challenging him soon.

A direct challenge did not concern him. Yet Karel knew that not all challenges were direct. Indirect assaults were the tools of a weaker foe—dishonorable, but all too often effective.

And Karel had too much to accomplish before he died. He had yet to see his disruptor room blast Earthers to oblivion. He had yet to take his revenge.

"I need you on the bridge as my personal guard," Klak said flatly. The second officer invited no dispute and Karel offered none.

The second officer had given him the truth about his brother's murder at the hands of the humans. He owed the Klingon something and Karel's family paid their debts, whether they were due in service or in blood.

When they arrived on the bridge, Commander Koloth was the only Klingon to note their arrival and shoot him a brief look from his weapons station. Karel looked with interest at the weapons console. It showed the status of both the port and starboard disruptor rooms, as well as surveillance images from each room.

Knowing he could not take time to indulge his curiosity now, Karel followed Klak to his station. The second officer's position was just behind the captain's chair, which was the most forward position on the bridge, or the ship for that matter. That way, the captain was the first to enter battle, or to face danger, or to seize a victory.

Klak sat in front of his console, which gave him immediate access to all major systems, as well as surveillance for—as far as Karel could tell—all areas of the ship. No wonder that Klak had seen Karel's fight with M'bac on the day of his promotion to senior weapons officer.

"Your first time on the bridge?" Klak said, though he already knew the answer. No officer of Karel's rank would be allowed on the bridge, unless he was a technician or the personal guard to either the captain or the second officer. There was an insinuation in Klak's question, and though Karel did not immediately understand Klak's intimation, he did not like the indirect communication.

In the end, he simply answered the question. "No."

"An ambitious warrior could learn much," Klak said. "And I think you will be particularly interested in the activities today."

At that point the doors to the bridge opened and the captain walked in with his two personal guards.

It was the first time Karel had seen the captain this close. The Klingon walked with great confidence and took his chair without giving Karel a glance. The captain's guards, however, did notice him and looked him over carefully, before taking standing positions on either side of the captain's chair.

Karel knew that the captain and the second officer were the only ones allowed personal guards on the bridge. They were also the only ones who needed guards, given the fact that they were the only ones likely to be challenged at their duty stations by their subordinates.

The guards allowed the captain and second officer to concentrate on their work, without constant threat of violent challenge to their authority by ambitious warriors.

The captain had some gray in his beard and hair, an open challenge to the truism that said "There are no old warriors." Though Karel had not seen him up close before, he knew the captain's record well.

Captain Kran was the veteran of many successful campaigns. In his almost twenty year career as captain he had tasted many victories, protecting the Empire against incursion and expanding its borders through conquest.

"Report," the captain said.

"We are approaching Federation space now," Klak said from his station.

Karel was suddenly alert. Since he was not a bridge officer, he was usually not privileged to know the ship's destination. Suddenly, his blood was alive with the nearness of the Earthers and of his revenge.

"Yes, your vengeance is near," Klak said. "And soon I will give you an opportunity to take it."

The second officer took a moment to appraise him. "I have seen you fight," he said. "Will you fight for me when the time comes? Will you fight for the right to take your vengeance?"

"Yes," Karel said.

"Tactical," the captain shouted.

Suddenly, two Klingon heavy cruisers appeared on the screen and Karel felt a wave of disappointment. It was only a drill, battle exercises. They were, however, very close to the Earthers. Perhaps that meant the *D'k tahg* would be going into battle for real shortly.

"Out of range," Klak said.

"Charge weapons," Captain Kran shouted.

Karel's mind went immediately to his disruptor room. His Klingons would perform well, even if the relief officer did not.

"Ready torpedoes," Kran said.

"Torpedoes?" Klak said. "Disruptor banks are standing by."

"Torpedoes," Kran repeated, scowling.

"Torpedoes, ready," Commander Koloth said.

Kevin Ryan

"Target each ship," Kran said. "Helm, prepare to use a warp burst to put us on top of them."

Karel wondered what the captain was planning. The range was too great for either torpedoes or disruptors.

"Fire torpedoes!" the captain shouted.

"Torpedoes away," Koloth said. "Detonating," he said a moment later, when the torpedoes exploded short of their targets.

"Helm, now," the captain said, and the *D'k tagh* flashed into warp, the stars on the main viewer flaring for an instant.

Afterward the *D'k tagh* returned to normal space, practically in top of the other Klingon vessels.

"Disruptors, now!" Captain Kran shouted.

Suddenly, Karel saw the brilliance of the maneuver. The early detonation of the torpedoes had temporarily overloaded the other ships' scanners. The captain had used the time to warp into position to fire the disruptors at nearly point-blank range.

The maneuver was new and very effective.

"Disruptors now," the captain called.

"Disruptors firing," Koloth replied almost before the captain had finished the command.

Karel saw the flash of green power and felt the energy of full disruptor fire vibrate through the deck.

But something was wrong. The port disruptor had not fired. The flash had appeared only on the starboard side. It was impossible.

Koloth's hands were quickly working his controls as he shouted into his console for a report from the relief officer.

"First target neutralized," Klak said.

Then the ship was rocked by fire. The second cruiser had opened fire, now with the same advantage of close range.

The captain was on his feet.

"Report," he shouted.

"Shields compromised. We have been neutralized. Simulation is ended," Klak announced.

"Damage," the captain called out.

Karel knew that drills were not full-power, but nor were they for display only as he knew human battle maneuvers were.

"Engineers have begun to repair shield damage," Klak said. Then the second officer manipulated his controls for a moment. "I will send another team to the port disruptor room."

Koloth stood. "The fault is mine, Captain. Permission to see the disruptor room for myself," he said.

The captain nodded, then let out a growl of displeasure.

Karel watched Koloth leave the bridge. Though Koloth had taken responsibility, Karel knew that the failure could not have been his fault. He also knew that the failure should have been impossible.

Then Klak rose to his feet next to Karel.

"We have done poorly," the second officer said. "There is no excuse for this failure of leadership."

The captain looked at Klak, frank surprise on his face, then understanding.

Suddenly, the bridge was completely quiet, as the Klingons there recognized the challenge for what it was.

Karel was instantly alert. As Klak's personal guard, the challenge was now his as well.

The response was immediate; one of the captain's

guards drew his blade, holding the *d'k tahg* in front of him as he charged. Karel reacted without thinking. He placed himself in front of Klak and deflected the knife with one hand as he struck a powerful blow with the other, hitting the Klingon square in the throat.

Then he turned, leaned in with his hip, and used the guard's momentum to hurl the Klingon to the deck. On the ground, the Klingon fought for breath, holding his damaged throat.

Karel immediately realized that the Klingon was no longer a threat. Nevertheless, he reached down and picked up his blade, which had fallen.

Now it was just the captain and his remaining guard facing Klak and Karel. It was a fair battle, yet Karel's blood screamed out a warning. There was something going on here that was not as simple as a challenge.

For the moment, there was no time to consider such subtleties. For now he had to concentrate on keeping himself alive.

The captain had his blade out, as did his guard. Karel held his own firmly and saw out of his peripheral vision that Klak was also ready.

Whatever happened would happen quickly now, while everyone's blood was hot.

The captain's guard was first to act. He looked at Klak for a moment, and then, instead of rushing forward to do battle, he turned to face the captain.

Captain Kran was caught by surprise for perhaps the first time in his career. It was also for the last time, Karel realized.

The large powerful guard brought down a fist on captain's hand—the one that held the blade.

As the blade fell to the ground, Klak rushed forward. The captain's guard grabbed him around the arm with one strong hand. Kran had just a moment to meet his guard's eyes before Klak reached him and the second officer's blade plunged into the captain's chest.

Captain Kran turned to face Klak, who merely sneered into his captain's face as he drove the *d'k tahg* in deeper, twisting it once the hilt touched the captain's uniform.

Captain Kran grunted once, and then his eyes closed and his service to the Empire was ended.

For a long moment, the bridge was completely quiet. The silence was broken by the sound of Klak's blade pulling free of Captain Kran's body.

The second officer—no, the *captain,* Karel reminded himself—stood and surveyed the bridge, challenging the other officers there with his eyes. Wiping the blade on Kran's uniform, he sat in the command chair.

He gave Karel a look telling him to take his position. The guard who had betrayed his charge was already standing at attention beside the new captain.

Karel did not hesitate. He walked over to Captain Kran's body and knelt down. He pried open the captain's eyes, lifted his head, and howled to let the next world know that a Klingon warrior was coming. He held the wail and then heard other voices from the bridge join his—though not, he noted, Klak's.

When that task was done, he took a position beside Klak. But he did so uneasily, with his blood calling out his shame.

What he had been part of today had not been an open challenge where true warriors used strength and cunning to determine leadership. Instead, he had been part of the worst kind of betrayal, where a warrior's trusted protector helped to murder him.

But there was even more to Klak's treachery than this, he realized. It was not an accident that Klak had chosen him as a personal guard today, just as it was not an accident that the port disruptor failed and started the cycle of events that led to a great warrior lying dead on the deck and a treacherous plotter sitting in his chair.

For now, Karel could do nothing to redeem the blow his honor had suffered, so he simply did his duty and stood guard over Captain Klak.

Chapter Nine

"SUBLIGHT SPEED, Mr. Sulu," Kirk said.

"Sublight, aye," Sulu said, and Kirk felt the vibration of the ship dropping out of warp speed. The captain noted that the vibration had been less strong than it ever had been in the past. Scotty must have upgraded inertial-dampening systems during his last round of repairs to the damage done by the Orions. He made a note to review the repair reports and commend the chief engineer.

"Do they see us, Mr. Spock?" Kirk asked.

"Negative, we are invisible to their satellite sensors as long as we keep at least one point five astronomical units away and remain in line with the system's star," Spock said.

Kirk nodded, studying the screen. The Orions had built their mining operation in a hurry, leaving gaps in their early-warning system. That left them vulnerable to the kind of surprise that Kirk was planning for them.

The ship and crew had endured too many surprises at the Orions' hands in the last two weeks. And while Kirk and crew had dealt out some surprises of their own, the captain was determined not to allow the Orions to catch up on that score.

"Did I mention that I don't like this?" Dr. McCoy said from his position behind Kirk's command chair.

"As a matter of fact, Doctor, you have talked about almost nothing else," Kirk said.

"Well, it hasn't seemed to do any good, Captain," McCoy said.

"On the contrary, Doctor, I have listened to every word you've said," Kirk replied.

"Before you decided to ignore me," McCoy countered.

The captain allowed himself a smile.

"At the very least, let me come with you," the doctor said.

"Unnecessary, Doctor. I do not plan on needing your services," Kirk said.

"You are leading a team into a fortified and heavily armed Orion complex. How do you intend to avoid needing my services, Captain?"

Kirk stood and gave the doctor another smile. "I intend to be careful."

He turned to his first officer. "Mr. Spock you have the bridge."

Kirk entered the turbolift and caught a glimpse at McCoy before the doors closed. The doctor was not pleased, but Kirk had refused to budge.

He had sent twenty-one people down to the second

planet of System 1324. Only nine had come back, and of those nine, Ensign McFadden later died of his injuries. In addition, the *Enterprise* had taken heavy damage. Only through luck and a series of Mr. Spock's and Scotty's miracles was it fully operational again.

This time, Kirk was not going to send anyone into danger in his place. And he was not going to risk the ship until he had found out exactly what it would be facing.

The mission still had dangers and he was still sending seven crew members into the unknown, but it was the right decision—he could feel it.

Kell and Benitez were the first to reach the armory, with the rest of the squad following in short order. Chief Fuller was there, as well as Lieutenant Commander Giotto and Chief Brantley.

"Mr. Anderson," Chief Brantley said, holding out a phaser rifle. Karel recognized the weapon. Captain Kirk had used it to save his life in the caves.

Taking the weapon, Kell noted that it was well balanced and had a satisfying weight to it. He wondered if the next time it was fired it would be at Captain Kirk. Next Brantley gave him a phaser 2 sidearm, and then proceeded to give out the same weapons to the rest of the squad.

"The captain wants you to take no chances," Security Chief Giotto said. "As you know, these rifles are significantly more powerful than your phaser-two weapons. They have also been specially modified to be more effective against Orion shields."

As the squad fell into line, Giotto looked to Fuller and said, "Give the word, Chief."

It was an unnecessary gesture. Chief Fuller was not

going on the mission and Chief Brantley was in command of the squad for its duration. But they were still Fuller's squad.

The chief looked them over and said simply, "Come back, all of you." Kell had been expecting a speech—something he had learned to expect from humans. "Now move out," Fuller said, his voice tight.

As the Klingon turned with the rest of the squad to follow Chief Brantley, he took one last look at Sam Fuller. It would no doubt be the last time he saw the human. He clearly saw pride in the chief's eyes as he took his own last look at his squad. The Klingon wondered what his expression would be when he learned of Kell's treachery against the captain.

The squad was silent all the way to the hangar bay—even Benitez was quiet.

Inside the hangar bay, the captain was waiting for them by the shuttlecraft. Its designation was *Galileo,* named, he knew, after an early human scientist.

When Kell first came on board, he had thought that the humans' pretense toward exploration and scientific study was one of their great deceptions. Now he knew this was not true. Humans lived by their principles, and died by them.

And while they valued peace and study, Kell had seen that the rest of the galaxy did not always cooperate. The Orions had recently forced the humans out of their complacency, and the Orions had paid the price for their presumptions.

The Empire was about to do the same. He wondered what price it would pay.

Even now, he could not believe that the Empire had

had anything to do with the recent Orion incident. He did not believe that Kirk would lie, but the human had provided no concrete proof, which meant Starfleet was relying on conjecture and intelligence. As a recent veteran of the Klingon intelligence division, Kell knew how unreliable that kind of information could be.

"We need to get under way immediately," Kirk said, gesturing for the squad to get inside.

As Kell stepped into the shuttle and took his seat, he realized he had been on a similar shuttle recently. A nearly identical craft had saved his life and likely the lives of all the humans on 1324's second planet. The boxy and inelegant shape belied the craft's true strength, he recognized.

Captain Kirk took the pilot's seat up front. Chief Brantley sat next to him, and the shuttle door closed. Through the forward window, Kell saw the clamshell doors at the end of the hangar bay begin to open.

At the same time, Kell could hear air being evacuated from the large bay. For the moment, the only thing between the shuttle and open space was an invisible forcefield. Finally, the sound of the air moving disappeared and the bay doors were open. There was a brief flash as the shield disappeared, and then the shuttle lifted off the deck.

The ride was much smoother than the brief trip he had taken in the heavily damaged shuttle on the planet. Kirk piloted with the easy confidence of someone who had had long practice.

The small craft shot forward and then they were in open space.

After a few moments, Kell saw the captain engage the shuttle's main engines and he knew that he was now racing toward his fate at nearly the speed of light.

Kell gripped the rifle on his lap firmly. He vowed that whatever his fate might be, he would meet it directly and without fear.

Even as the shock of what he was seeing registered in his mind, Justman found himself doing his job. Using tactical sensors, he plotted the trajectory of each of the Starfleet officers as they shot through space, completely unprotected from the harsh vacuum.

He was feeding the data to the science station as the captain called out, "Get me transporters online now. Mr. Justman, fire phasers at the Klingon vessel. Pick your targets."

Justman knew that torpedoes would be more effective, but they posed too great a risk to the Starfleet officers in space, who still had a chance. Contrary to what many civilians believed, humans could survive in the vacuum of space for brief periods. He also knew, however, that the survival time was measured in seconds.

"We have a transporter lock on six," Science Officer Okuda said.

"Helm, evasive maneuvers. Justman, drop shields now," the captain barked.

Even as he did so, Lieutenant Commander Justman knew the danger of dropping the shields with hostile ships in range, but they had no choice. He hit the switch without hesitation.

As he did, he felt the pull of high-speed impulse maneuvers, which put more of a strain on artificial gravity and inertial compensators than anything else the ship did. Grabbing his console for support, Justman tracked the Klingon cruisers on his display.

"Klingons powering weapons," he called out.

Then Okuda's voice called out, "We've got them. Getting lock on more survivors."

"Raise shields," Captain Rodriguez said.

Justman did and the shields came on an instant before the Klingon ship fired. He saw the shield indicator light come on, and waited for the inevitable impact of Klingon disruptor fire.

It did not come.

A glance at his screen told him why. Two full-powered disruptor blasts tore into the fourteen Starfleet officers floating in space. He didn't have to check his sensors to see that there was nothing there to scan. His eyes told him that the fourteen people had been instantly disintegrated.

Then he realized that the blasts were just a decoy. The other Klingon cruiser powered another weapon.

"Incoming torpedoes!" Justman shouted.

"Evasive," the captain called, and Justman felt the ship lurch violently to the side. There were four torpedoes. Though they were guided weapons that could track a ship with deadly accuracy, they also moved very fast and the magnetic containment system that separated the matter from the antimatter would operate for only a short period of time.

Thus, if a missile did not hit almost immediately, it would detonate harmlessly in space. Justman tracked the missiles carefully as they tried to follow the *Yorkshire* as it ran through its evasive maneuvers.

The first torpedo was a clean miss. So was the second. The third detonated close enough to rock the *Yorkshire*. Then the fourth made a direct hit on the aft shield.

Justman checked his readout. The shield was holding.

Shields would not take many more direct hits, but for now they were nearly at full power.

"Return fire, Mr. Justman, concentrate on the lead ship and hit them hard," Captain Rodriguez said.

Justman watched the helm's maneuvers carefully and tried to anticipate the *Yorkshire*'s next move to give the torpedoes the best chance of finding their targets.

One torpedo was away. Then another.

He waited for the reload time. It was just seconds, but it seemed like an eternity. Then two more torpedoes were away.

One of them hit their mark almost directly on the lead Klingon cruiser. The other torpedo struck the ship a glancing blow.

"Status of the survivors. Did we get them?" the captain called out.

"Sickbay reports that they are treating four of the *Endeavor*'s crew," the communications officer said. "Two didn't make it."

And fourteen more were disintegrated in space, Justman thought, knowing that the rest of the bridge crew was having the same thought.

"Shield status," the captain said.

"Shields at over ninety percent," Justman said.

"No damage reported," the communications officer said.

"Mr. Okuda, what about the Klingons?" the captain asked.

"Their shields have lost some power and I'm reading fluctuations that suggest some damage on board the lead cruiser."

Justman checked his readouts. "Their weapons systems are at full power but they are maintaining position."

"Ready weapons, I'll need phasers and torpedoes on my command," Rodriguez said.

"Captain, we're being hailed," the communications officer said.

"Audio only," the captain said.

"Earther commander," said the voice of the Klingon captain. "You simply drag out the inevitable. Watch the *Endeavor* and see your own future."

The main viewer trained on the *Endeavor*. Justman could once again see the airlock doors open and the frightened faces of the people inside.

"Stop this!" Rodriguez shouted. "I demand—"

"They've broken the connection," the communications officer said.

The bridge fell silent as all eyes went to the screen. The crew waited for the inevitable. Justman knew they would not have to wait long.

Chapter Ten

IT OCCURRED TO KELL that he could end Captain Kirk's life and his own mission right there in the shuttle. He was holding a high-powered phaser and was sitting less than three meters behind the human. The Starfleet officers around him trusted him and would never be able to stop him in time.

Yet the Klingon knew the would not do it. The first time he was alone with the captain was in the briefing room on his first day aboard the *Enterprise*. He did not do it then because a warrior defeated a foe face-to-face.

Much had changed in the short weeks since then, and Kell knew now that his entire mission for the Empire compromised his honor. Yet there were some compromises he would not make. When the time came to kill Captain Kirk, he would do it face-to-face.

"Approaching range of surveillance satellites," Chief

Brantley announced, quickly working the navigation controls.

"Reducing speed," the captain said, and Kell felt the slight shudder of sublight deceleration.

"Course plotted. Nearest satellite moving out of range...now," Brantley said.

Kirk executed another maneuver. He alternately sped up and turned to stay out of range of the Orions' early-warning system. With the satellites orbiting quickly around the planet, the sensor coverage changed constantly.

Plotting a course through such a mess was very difficult. Piloting that course was nearly impossible. Yet Brantley and Kirk were doing it as if it were a matter of routine.

Finally, Kell felt the engines' hum increase in pitch and watched as the planet grew quickly in front of them.

The world was blue and white. Kell wondered if there was any land at all. There was certainly none that he could see on the quarter view that showed through the forward window.

"Entering planet's outer atmosphere," Kirk said, as he worked the controls. "Brace yourselves, we're going to be heading for the surface at high speed. Then we have to come around at low altitude. It may get bumpy."

A sudden glow against the shuttle's forward shields told Kell they had made contact with the atmosphere. The glow quickly brightened and the Klingon could feel the rumble of the shuttle's movement through atmosphere.

In seconds the glow became a fireball that Kell knew was leading the ship, held away from the hull by the shuttle's force screens. When the glow became painfully bright, Chief Brantley hit a switch and the blast doors covered the window.

The shuttle was now hurtling at high speed toward the surface, with the captain using instruments to control its descent.

The rumble grew, shaking the Klingon in his seat. Then Kell pitched forward as the captain executed a sudden deceleration and the flight became smooth again. When the blast shields opened, he could see blue sky. From his angle he could not see the planet's surface, but he assumed they were at a fairly low altitude.

Now, Kell knew, came the longest part of the trip. Since the shuttle came down on the far side of the planet to avoid detection, it would have to travel thousands of kilometers to reach the Orion installation. Even at hypersonic speeds, that would take some time.

"I can't believe you are going to just sit there and wait," McCoy blustered from behind Spock. It occurred to the Vulcan once more that it was neither necessary nor logical for the ship's surgeon to spend so much of his time on the bridge. On the other hand, it was standard practice on board the *Enterprise*. Failure to accept that fact of his life among humans would be illogical.

"What part do you find difficult to believe, Doctor? That a Vulcan would be able to sit patiently when patience is required, or that I would follow the captain's orders?" Spock replied.

"There must be something else we can do," McCoy said, ignoring him.

Spock gave the doctor's words some thought. Humans seemed to need to remain active, even when activity could not further their cause at the moment.

The Vulcan knew the doctor was motivated by concern for the captain and the landing party. He also knew that McCoy was not the only one concerned. Subtle changes in body language told him that the bridge crew was anxious.

And Mr. Scott was at his station despite the fact that he had not been scheduled for bridge duty.

As a Vulcan, he did not require pointless activity to keep his mind free of anxiety. Worry would not help the captain. Focusing his mind on other things was simply a matter of mental discipline.

Yet he judged that it would be simpler to give the crew a task than it would be to teach the four hundred and twenty-four of them even rudimentary Vulcan mental disciplines.

"Mr. Scott, can you recalibrate sensors to track the shuttle on the ground?" Spock said.

The chief engineer shook his head. "At this range...I will see if I can," Mr. Scott said, sitting at his console.

"Lieutenant Uhura, can you boost reception strength so we can monitor the landing party's communicator exchanges?" Spock asked.

"Sir, at this range, we will only be able to hear them if they use the shuttle's com system," she said. "The individual communicators are too low in power...unless we used spectral analysis of the upper atmosphere to look for resonating frequencies. It would mean reprogramming astrological sensors," she said.

"Then you had better begin," Spock said.

"And we might have to move the ship around the system to find the best signal," she said.

"Coordinate with the helm, Lieutenant," Spock said.

The Vulcan looked at doctor McCoy, who did not

look happy, but he had ceased complaining. Spock judged that a small victory.

He heard Mr. Scott mutter in rather colorful language. The volume was too low for the humans to hear, yet Spock heard it clearly.

Finally, Mr. Scott stood up and headed for the turbolift. "I will be down at sensor control," he said.

The engineer's voice was gruff but Spock knew that he was pleased to have an activity. The Vulcan thought that his and Lieutenant Uhura's projects might even prove useful.

For himself, he preferred using mental discipline to keep from nonproductive worry over the captain. It was a simple matter of focusing his mental energy on useful tasks. At the moment, he created several scenarios for potential dangers to the captain and the landing party. He ran through each scenario, calculating the *Enterprise*'s best possible response to each. To be certain of his results, he ran and reran each scenario over and over.

Spock judged that a useful task, a much better use of his time and mental energy than human worry.

Kell did not mind the monotony. He knew it defined battle almost as much as actual conflict. As a young Klingon, he had dreamt of endless battles and victories. Now he knew that even the most intense fighting was usually a short diversion from the duty that took most of a warrior's time—waiting for the next battle.

For now he was content to wait. And he was grateful for the silence that his squad seemed to be respecting. The Klingon doubted that he would survive long after killing Kirk. Kell recognized that this was likely the last similar period of rest that he would have.

And while he was prepared to face his duty and his own death, at the moment he was not prepared to face Leslie Parrish. She would never understand why anything further was impossible for him. She would find out soon enough. In the meantime, he did not want to see her disappointment in her face. He saw too much of his own dishonor there.

Finally, the captain said, "Take over, Mr. Brantley," then got up to face the security squad.

"We will be approaching the Orion mining operation shortly. Our initial mission will be reconnaissance only. We are not to engage the enemy unless they leave us no choice," Kirk said.

Kell felt the comfortable weight of the phaser rifle on his lap. The captain had ordered the weapons come with them on this mission. He wondered if Kirk actually believed the landing party would be able to avoid *engaging* the Orions for long.

"Our primary mission will be to collect data on the installation, determine if there are any ships on the ground or any defenses that might pose a threat to the *Enterprise*. We are also to evaluate the nature of the threat the Orions pose to the indigenous population. If possible, we are to avoid all contact with the planet's natives. They are a pretechnological society and are not ready for contact with a warp-capable society."

"Excuse me, sir," Benitez said, "but haven't they most likely already had some contact with the Orions?"

"Probably, yes," Kirk replied. "The Orions are not known for their strict adherence to the Prime Directive.

Nevertheless, while we cannot solve all the problems in the galaxy, we can avoid adding to them."

"Approaching landing site," Brantley said.

Kirk turned around and took his seat. "Thank you, Mr. Brantley. I will take it from here."

A few minutes later, the Klingon could see the tops of trees—the first sign of the surface he had seen since they entered the atmosphere. The ship slowed and Kell felt the main engines disengage and the antigravity system take over.

Kirk quickly piloted them to a soft landing. Kell could now see trees and hills in the distance. From what he could tell, they had put down in a forest.

Kirk and Brantley stood up and the security team followed suit. Suddenly, the unspoken agreement to keep silent was broken. Predictably, it was Benitez who broke it.

"What do you think, Flash, piece of cake?" the human said, smiling and holding up his phaser rifle.

"If that," Kell said, returning the smile.

Kell also made a point of catching Leslie's eyes. He did not know what would happen when they went outside, and he wanted to leave her with something. When she looked his way, he smiled, and was surprised to see her return the gesture.

Then Kirk opened the door and stepped outside. The security team filed out behind him.

In the open air, the Klingon saw they were indeed in a forest, a thick one. In fact, Kirk had somehow guided the shuttle under a canopy of green trees, effectively hiding it from the air.

Kirk turned to the security team and said, "This way," then led them to the Orion installation.

They had not gotten two meters before the ground started to tremble beneath Kell's feet. The trembling soon turned to a shaking of the ground.

"Stay near the shuttle," Kirk said. He headed back himself.

Before the squad had taken position, the ground was shaking violently. Kell was only able to keep his feet by holding on to the shuttle, which was also pitching.

A nearly deafening roar filled the air, accompanying the shaking.

The siege lasted perhaps two minutes, then quickly dissipated.

The squad stood up straight and looked to the captain.

"It's the mining," Parrish said, studying her tricorder.

Kirk nodded, "I think we have detected *a significant threat to the indigenous population.*"

Chapter Eleven

AT THE END OF his duty shift on the bridge, Karel went immediately to the port disruptor room. The relief weapons officer lay dead on the floor, a bloody wound showing through his uniform.

Command Koloth was leaning over a console when Karel walked in, but turned to look him over carefully.

"The *malfunction* has been repaired," Koloth said with disgust in his voice. Then the commander walked up to Karel.

"I had to relieve him," he said, pointing to the dead Klingon on the floor. "Seems he was bad for efficiency." Then Koloth looked straight into Karel's eyes. "Are you bad for efficiency, Senior Weapons Officer Karel?"

Karel understood the real question that Koloth was asking. *Would you sabotage your own weapons room?* Or more specifically, *Do you have any honor?*

His response came out as a snarl. "I serve the Empire with my blood and with my honor."

After he finished speaking, Karel realized that Koloth's question was a fair one, given the events of the day. Yet, the commander seemed satisfied with his response and backed off slightly.

"I see you also serve *Captain* Klak," Koloth said. "Can you do both?"

It was another good question, one for which Karel had no answer. It was also bold on Koloth's part. Like all parts of the ship, the disruptor room was under constant surveillance. Klak would want complete loyalty from his officers, particularly his bridge crew.

Then Karel understood that Koloth knew this and did not care. He had no doubt been loyal to Captain Kran, who now lay dead on the bridge, betrayed by his personal guard and murdered by Klak.

If one of Kran's guards was already loyal to Klak, Karel wondered why the Klingon had wanted him on the bridge. Up until now, he had thought it was to get him out of the disruptor room so the relief officer could perform whatever form of sabotage was required to give Klak a pretense by which to challenge Kran.

Now Karel wondered if there was another reason. Had Klak wanted him on the bridge to deal with Koloth, if the officer tried to help his captain?

Had Koloth surprised Klak by heading immediately to the disruptor room? Was Koloth meant to die at Karel's hand on the bridge with Kran?

But Koloth was still alive, and the relief officer who had performed the sabotage was dead. The matter between Klak and Koloth was far from settled.

"I am finished here," Koloth said. Then he leaned in close to Karel and said, "The warrior who seeks favor over victory will usually find neither."

They were the words of Kahless the Unforgettable and the sound of them shamed Karel after his role in Klak's murder—for it was a murder.

Then Koloth was gone and Karel watched as the warriors on the evening duty cycle began their maintenance.

Karel headed back to his quarters. He had much to consider. The matter between Klak and Koloth still needed to be settled. Karel's blood told him that he would soon have to choose between his commanding officer and his captain.

The group moved as quickly as they could through the dense forest.

"Sir," Parrish said. "I have something."

She immediately had Kirk's attention. "It's a group of humanoids, moving that way," she said, pointing. "There is also some heavy equipment in the area. Might be Orion."

"Come on," Kirk said leading the way.

The landing party headed out at a run, dodging trees as they moved.

Kirk was in the lead and the Klingon realized once again that he could take a shot now and end his mission. Once again, he dismissed the thought. He would not shoot the human in the back. The time for Kirk's death would come soon enough.

The last time the *Enterprise*'s security forces took on the Orions they had lost more people than were on this current mission. And this time they were facing a larger, more fortified installation.

Kell realized that the Orions might well do his work for him, but dismissed the thought as unworthy of a Klingon warrior. He would do his own killing.

And he would do it soon.

For now, he was content to follow the captain. Perhaps he could settle some debts with the Orions as a last honorable act.

Kell noticed they were heading up a rise that became gradually steeper. He watched as Kirk came to a sudden stop at the top of the rise. The others did the same.

Kell and Benitez came to a stop together, looking down into a ravine. It was thirty to forty meters down and fairly steep, with another similar slope opposite their position. There must have once been a river or large stream cutting through here, he realized.

It would have been a long time ago, however, because now the ground was dry and full of trees. And at the bottom of the ravine a single humanoid was running for his life.

Kell watched the humanoid zigzag; then he saw an energy bolt crash into the ground a few meters from the figure, creating a crater about two meters across. Tracing back about forty meters, the Klingon saw the source of the blast. He recognized it instantly. It was an Orion flying weapons platform, skimming two to three meters off the ground.

The device was oval in shape, a little more than two meters in width. An armored console rose out of the front and carried the cannon that was now spewing deadly fire against a single, unarmed primitive. Kell's blood burned with anger as he watched the platform fire again, and again. The Orion was wearing an armored suit that hid his face.

The shots missed the running person, who dodged nimbly, using trees as cover. The platform, however, had trouble navigating around the trees. Kell shook his head. The Orion was a fool to take such a heavy weapon into a forest environment.

The Orions had done many foolish things during the System 1324 incident. Yet they had killed fourteen better warriors before they had been defeated.

And as clumsy as the platform was in the forest, it still was a powerful weapon. And Kell knew that a powerful weapon in the hands of a fool could still do a lot of damage.

At the moment, however, the Orion was succeeding in damaging only trees and ground. A blast hit one tree squarely, obliterating its trunk and sending it crashing down.

The falling tree almost accomplished what the energy cannon could not. The humanoid figure barely leapt out of the way of the falling trunk.

The shield of the platform flared often as it made constant contact with low-hanging branches of the nearby trees.

Nevertheless, the Orion was closing the distance between the platform and the running figure. Kell saw that it was just a matter of time.

Chief Brantley spoke the Klingon's next thought aloud.

"Captain, request permission to intercede," he said.

Kirk who was studying the scene carefully, raised one hand and said, "Not yet."

"Sir, the Prime Directive does not—"

"It's not the Prime Directive, Mr. Brantley. There's something else going on here," Kirk said.

Then Kell saw the Orion shield shimmer for a moment, and he realized that the Orion must have turned it off, because it stopped flaring against nearby branches.

The move made sense, because the Orion was able to increase his speed and close more of the distance between himself and the runner.

Then the rocks began to fly.

To Kell, they seemed to come from nowhere. At least six good-sized rocks sailed through the air. All of them made contact with either the weapons platform or the armored figure driving it. The Orion was battered by three of the projectiles but kept his hands on the controls.

Then the Klingon saw where the rocks had come from. On his side of the ravine, the Klingon could see three figures about midway down and several meters over. They had been invisible before. But now they had revealed themselves and were pitching rock after rock at the Orion.

On the other side, the Klingon saw that there were three more figures doing the same.

Now the running person was almost directly below the landing party's position. He was also in the open, since the trees gave way to a clearing there.

The figure did something that surprised Kell. He turned and faced the Orion platform, standing still and seeming to dare the Orion to get him.

The Orion seemed determined to do just that. He barreled on ahead. And though he was no longer navigating through trees, he now had to contend with hurled rocks. They struck the platform and the pilot's armored suit regularly as it lurched toward its prey. The whole scene took on a pattern that seemed almost familiar to the Klingon.

It almost looked like the pincer formation Klingons used to hunt *targs*. The primitive who had been chased was at the apex, while the others weakened or distracted the Orion.

And while the Orion pilot's armored suit was protecting him from serious harm, the rocks had the effect of making his aim go wide. Yet the Orion tried to remain focused and kept up a barrage of fire from his cannon.

Another shot came dangerously close to the primitive who was his target. Yet the humanoid stood perfectly still, again seeming to dare the Orion to come closer.

The Orion complied. He was no more than ten meters from his target, trying to get a lock on the humanoid.

That target removed something from his belt. He moved with a calm deliberateness that spoke of great confidence, determination, and a complete fearlessness.

The Klingon thought it would be a shame to watch this person die.

Then his companions let loose with a new volley of rocks, making the pilot reel from the blows. The Klingon realized something important. The Orion had never turned his shield back on. He had been completely focused on his prey and that prey's challenge.

The Orion got off his closest shot yet. It struck barely two meters from the humanoid, who ignored the dirt that the blast threw at him.

He seemed to be waiting for his moment. He lifted his left hand quickly and the barrage of rocks stopped. Then his right hand was a blur of motion. Kell caught a very quick glimpse of what looked like a small axe. Then the weapon went flying through the air, end over end.

It caught the Orion right below the helmet and above armored chest plating. Reflexively, the pilot reached for the axe, which seemed embedded fairly deeply into the suit and into the Orion within it. The Orion began to flail and Kell realized that the humanoid had struck it a killing blow.

One hand got a firm grip on the handle, but the disoriented Orion stumbled back and then pitched off the side of the platform. It was two meters to the ground. The pilot hit hard and was still. Kell was certain that the Orion was dead.

Incredible, the Klingon thought. Seven primitives hunted and bested the same type of Orion platform that had taken so many of his comrades on the last mission. And those fallen humans had not lacked either in courage or in resourcefulness.

The humanoid rushed to the Orion, presumably to confirm that he was dead.

"Sir," Kell heard Parrish call out. "Sir, I'm reading two more of those."

Kirk was instantly alert, scanning the ravine with his eyes. Kell did the same. This time he saw the first platform before it began to fire.

The first blast scattered the group of primitives.

Kirk didn't hesitate. "Let's move. Engage and neutralize the weapons."

"Prime Directive, sir?" Brantley said. Kell could hear the smile in the chief's voice.

"Try to keep a low profile," Kirk said.

Then the captain headed down the ravine at a run, his

phaser rifle out and ready to fire. Kell gripped his own rifle firmly and followed.

Justman looked again at the airlock on the *Endeavor*'s main hull. Once again, he could see frightened human faces inside. Those officers must have known what was coming; yet they were not panicked.

Even as he recoiled inside from the brutality of the Klingon captain's ploy, he had to admit that it was effective. The Klingon had released twenty unprotected humans into space, forcing the *Yorkshire* to drop its shields to try to recover them.

The Klingons had fired, but the *Yorkshire* had been able to lock on to six of the survivors and get the shields back on before the Klingon weapons found their mark. Even now, Justman's readouts told him that the shields were almost back to one hundred percent.

Now, the Klingons were about to send twenty more humans into space. Justman looked at the captain. He also saw through the ploy.

Trying to recover the humans would be foolish. It was what the Klingons expected. It was also the only course Captain Rodriguez would take.

That was what made him the Captain, and in that moment Lieutenant Commander Justman felt a deep pride. The captain would not abandon who he was because of the Klingons, or of any danger.

Could even the fierce Klingon warriors say that? Justman felt the captain's resolve and confidence radiate from the man. He decided that the Klingons were fools for betting against Captain Rodriguez.

"Airlock opened," Science Officer Okuda said. Justman was sure that he was hearing the captain's confidence speaking through the science officer's calm voice.

The captain ordered evasive maneuvers, and then Justman heard the order he knew was coming.

"Drop shields," Rodriguez said. "Fire phasers." Then he heard, "I want transporters, now!"

Justman's hands moved more quickly than he would have thought capable and he was certain that it was the captain's force of will that was guiding them. As he watched the shield indicator lights go off, he felt the deck lurch under his feet.

Ignoring the shuddering of the ship, he targeted the lead ship, choosing the weakest point he could find in their shields—right above the starboard nacelle. The red beams found their mark, but before his mind registered the hit, he was firing at another weak spot on the long neck of the cruiser.

Another blast, then another.

Then the warning light told him the Klingons had achieved a weapons lock, despite their helmsman's aggressive maneuvers.

Before he could announce it, the captain was shouting for him to raise shields. His hands complied with the order before it was complete. Yet, even so, he saw it was going to be close.

Then his readout told him both Klingon ships were firing disruptors.

It was going to be *very* close.

Before the shields were fully up, he felt the ship rock violently under his feet. Three of the four Klingon disruptor blasts hit the *Yorkshire* directly on the primary hull.

The shields had been perhaps at thirty percent at the time of the hit. They had provided some protection but not enough.

Justman received his first indication of the damage nearly immediately, when the panel in front of him exploded in a flash of sparks. Reflexively, he pulled his hands away.

It took a moment for his vision to clear after the blast. When it did, he saw the captain leaning over Science Officer Okuda's console, listening to damage reports.

"Are you okay, Mr. Justman?" the captain asked.

"Yes, sir," Justman said, trying to keep his voice even. Then he was surveying the damage to his weapons console.

"Report," the captain said.

"The phaser control circuits are fried," he said. "The phaser room responds that the system checks out okay, but the bridge relay circuits are out. Shields and torpedoes are still online. I've got shields up to sixty percent now, sir."

Okuda and the communications officer were giving their reports as well. Damage was relatively light.

"Sickbay has twelve survivors, sir," the com officer announced.

Justman did not have to look up to see the captain's smile. He felt it rising on his own face.

"Shield power is down on lead Klingon cruiser," Okuda announced. "Significantly."

"Hail them," Rodriguez said.

"No response," the reply came.

"Mr. Justman, head down to auxiliary control," Captain Rodriguez said. "We need those phasers back on-line."

"Aye, sir," Justman said. As he turned to go, the captain took his position at the weapons console. He spared Justman a grim smile and said, "Good work."

Then the captain was absorbed in the console's readouts and Justman was racing for the turbolift.

He made it to auxiliary control quickly and found it bustling with activity, with the junior communications officer and engineering officer and computer control officer conferring with the bridge and other areas of the ship.

He relieved the very nervous junior lieutenant at the auxiliary weapons console, which was a nearly exact duplicate of the one on the bridge. Except that this one was undamaged.

He traced the damage-control circuits and called down to the phaser room. He had to reroute the circuit while keeping the system hot and ready to fire. It was exacting work, and he knew he had to do it quickly.

"Mr. Justman, report," the captain's voice said, his calm, confident tones giving Justman more confidence.

Without stopping his work, Justman said, "I'll have it in a second, Captain."

"The Klingons aren't talking, we think they're preparing another group..." Rodriguez said.

Justman knew what that meant. The *Yorkshire* couldn't use torpedoes so close to the unprotected humans floating in space. And they needed weapons fire to give them precious seconds to maneuver and avoid the Klingon blasts while the shields were down.

"Got it," Justman said. He knew he had cut a few corners and he knew that the chief engineer would not approve of his work, yet he was equally sure that the circuit would hold.

Before the captain broke the communication, Justman heard enough bridge chatter to know that the Klingons had forced another group of humans into space.

Justman's panel told him the captain was firing the phasers. Then the ship shook under his feet, announcing the maneuvers as his indicators told him the shields were down.

Then the tactical readout in front of him told Justman that the Klingons had a weapons lock—much faster than last time, he noted.

Then the officer at the engineering console was shouting behind him that they had an overload in helm control.

What happened next happened very quickly.

The ship veered sharply, and Justman was thrown with great force onto the floor. *That was not just an aggressive evasion maneuver,* he thought.

Then he felt what only could have been an explosion rock the ship.

Before that thought had completely registered, he was on his feet and at his console. He saw that shields were down.

"Does the transporter room have anyone?" he barked.

The communication's officer's shaky voice came back with, "They have a signal, but they're having trouble..." the officer said.

Justman called up a transporter status readout on his panel. Someone in the transporter room was struggling to resolve a transporter signal. The ship must have been hit while a group of survivors were in midtransport.

He tried to raise the bridge. No response.

Then he saw it. The helm was offline and the Kling-ons had another weapons lock.

Shields were still down.

Transporters were still engaged.

Justman knew he could not afford to hesitate and he did not, though he would replay the moment in his nightmares for the rest of his life.

With a single touch, he brought the shields up and ended the lives of six human beings still in the trans-porter beam.

Aiming the phasers manually, he targeted the lead ship. He watched the twin phaser beams strike the Klingon ship's starboard nacelle. Then he watched the shield protecting the nacelle flare brightly for a moment before it failed.

He knew he had a clear shot at the nacelle and he took it.

The cruiser was veering off to protect the unshielded yet vital part of the ship.

The maneuver was executed quickly and it was almost fast enough. Fortunately, Justman was faster and saw the beam strike the nacelle a glancing but solid blow.

He saw one phaser beam tear through hull and watched pieces of nacelle fly into space.

At best, the Klingon would lose warp capability and a fair amount of its power. At worst, they would be fight-ing a warp-core breach.

Both cruisers withdrew and Justman allowed himself a single deep breath.

He confirmed the shields were up—and at better than fifty percent. Then he tried the bridge and couldn't get a signal.

He turned to the communications officer.

"I need the bridge, now," he said.

The lieutenant at the console worked his controls and said, "I can't reach the bridge, the circuit must have been damaged."

Justman walked to the communications console and tried it himself. No signal.

"I'm also having trouble getting damage-control reports from some sectors of the primary hull," the communications officer said.

Justman nodded. They must have taken the hit somewhere in the primary hull. That would explain the cut communications lines.

Without communications to the bridge, Justman would not know how to help the captain. And given the pounding they had just taken, Captain Rodriguez would need auxiliary systems.

A flash of insight told him what to do.

"Can you tie into the *Endeavor*'s viewer and show me the damage?" Justman asked the officer.

He put a hand on the com officer's shoulder. The junior lieutenant was young. What was his name?

"Mr. Heller, can you tie us in?" Justman said.

"Yes, sir," the young officer said. He called up the access codes on a display and punched them in. "I'm in their system...now."

"Good, show me our primary hull. Put it on the viewer," Justman said.

Justman turned to the auxiliary-control viewscreen, and sensed that all of the other officers in the room were doing the same.

The first image of the *Yorkshire* was distant. The

ship looked intact, but there was some scoring on the upper section of the hull. They would need a closer look.

"Magnify, focus on upper half of primary hull," Justman said.

He heard the click of controls and watched the screen as the image rippled, then shifted.

An instant later, he saw the upper portion of the hull. The image was very clear, but what it showed him was completely impossible.

He blinked and looked again, waiting for his vision to clear.

But the image refused to change.

Then he knew there was no mistake. He was sure.

The bridge of the *U.S.S. Yorkshire* was gone, obliterated along with part of the deck below it.

Chapter Twelve

CAPTAIN KIRK WAS the first to fire. He took the shot running, about midway down the wall of the ravine.

It was a difficult shot, but the captain did not miss.

The powerful phaser beam leapt from the rifle and reached out for the pilot's head. It flared brilliantly against the weapons platform's shield. Kell felt a tinge of disappointment. Unlike the first pilot, this one had not turned off his shield.

If the shield were off, this battle would already be half over.

Kirk had no doubt studied the reports from the System 1324 incident, which showed that the shield was weakest at the top.

Kell was not surprised to see the shield holding, even after a phaser rifle blast. He had seen the platform's shields absorb beam after beam of phaser-2 fire.

They would absorb more than one blast from a phaser rifle.

But not much more.

Kell fired his own weapon. The blast went wide and he aimed for another shot, targeting the weapons platform in the rear this time. He hit that shield at the pilot's chest level. The shield flared a brilliant purple.

Kirk came to a stop about two-thirds of the way down the ravine. The cover was adequate there with more trees than the bare clearing directly below them.

Kell saw movement in his peripheral vision and guessed that the primitives were escaping behind them. He kept up the fire. He and Benitez concentrated on the platform in the rear, while the captain and most of the others concentrated on the one on the front.

The pilots were slow to respond. They expected to be hunting unarmed primitive beings and were now being pounded by high-powered phaser fire on a planet that should have contained no technology beyond simple hand tools.

Few beings would be able to adapt quickly to that abrupt a development. Clearly, the Orions were not among that few; they were buffeted by fire. They fired their own weapons but could not find decent targets and none of the deadly blasts came anywhere near the landing party's position.

"Hold your fire," Kirk called out, after a few moments.

He stepped down to get closer to the bottom of the ravine. Taking careful aim, he fired two blasts at the lead platform. Then another three at the rear vehicle. Both ships' shields flared and then disappeared, though the vehicles were left intact and the pilots unharmed.

Kirk started down the ravine wall. Chief Brantley called out to him.

"Captain, the last time we faced those weapons platforms, they were booby-trapped. The Orions did not want to be taken alive."

Kirk nodded, but continued down, saying, "They knew they would be taking on Starfleet then. This time they weren't expecting any resistance, and the Orions don't usually resort to that kind of extreme action. I'm betting that they didn't institute the same protocols here. They still think this is a secret operation."

Then he shot the security team a look over his shoulder. "And nobody blows themselves up until I get some answers."

Kirk stepped out into the clearing, his rifle aimed straight at the Orions.

"This is Captain James T. Kirk, of the *Starship Enterprise*. You are under arrest under more Federation and Starfleet articles than I have time to name. Take your hands off the controls of your vehicle."

The Orions complied, raising their hands.

By then, the security squad had followed Chief Brantley to the clearing. Kell noticed that there was no sign of the primitives. He found himself scanning carefully, covering the captain's position. He quickly realized the irony of trying to protect the man he intended to kill. Yet it did not stop him from doing his job. He would continue to do that job until it came time to do his final duty for the Empire.

"Take off the helmets. Let me see you," Kirk said.

Kell knew there was no tactical reason to give that order. Yet he understood why Kirk did it. The Orions had done much killing from behind their masks and protected weapons.

Such was not the way of true Klingon warriors. Nor was it, Kell had learned, the way of human beings.

Now it would no longer be an option for the honorless Orions, who slowly removed their helmets, revealing their green faces.

The two pilots were large, even by Orion standards. But these two pilots did not look very fierce out of their masks with a high-powered phaser weapon pointed straight at their heads.

Holding the rifle firm, Kirk said, "Now we are going to have a little talk about your operation here."

The Orions did not even make a pretense of defiance. They were frightened, and by the way Kirk was looking at them, Kell thought they had good reason to be.

"Let's start with who you are working for," the captain said.

Before either of the aliens could respond, a bolt of energy tore into the ground behind and to the right of Captain Kirk.

Kell turned his head reflexively, making sure that no one in the squad was hit. Parrish was safe. As was Benitez and the others.

Then his eyes shot forward again and he saw another blast tear their way.

"I've got two more coming in!" Parrish shouted.

Kell could see them in the distance, lumbering along.

"Prepare to fall back," Kirk ordered.

"Sir, I show two more behind us," Parrish's voice said.

"Anderson, Benitez, Jawer, stay with the captain,"

Chief Brantley called out. "The rest of you come with me."

Brantley would cover the rear, but Kell knew they were in trouble. They were in the open with two of the Orion vehicles on either side.

They had taken down two Orion platforms earlier, but they had done that from covered positions and they had had the advantage of surprise.

One of the prisoners smiled, though it looked to Kell more like a sneer. Then a bolt of energy tore over his shoulder and hit a few meters from Kell's position.

"Down," the captain yelled, firing his phaser at the distant Orion vehicles. The two prisoners smiled broadly now, until a bolt shot uncomfortably close to them. As Kell fired his own weapon, he saw the realization dawn on the Orions' faces: they were in danger, standing up and caught in the crossfire between the Orion and Starfleet fire.

Before they could drop, the one on the right caught a blast in the center of the back from one of the Orion platforms. His partner looked on in horror as the Orion was vaporized, for a moment distracted from the reality of his own danger.

Then another blast caught him and he disappeared in a flash of energy.

Kell fired. He judged that they would be able to eliminate the four platforms but resigned himself to the notion that most of the landing party would not survive the encounter. The faces of his section mates and one face in particular rose in his mind. He forced them back by sheer will. No one would survive if everyone did not remain focused.

He heard the battle raging behind him and wondered how Chief Brantley and the others were faring. Suddenly, the battle sounded horrific, loud and even more intense than the one he, Kirk, and the others were fighting.

Two explosions sounded in rapid succession. Then, most of the sound behind him died away and he heard another sound that chilled him: an Orion blast fired from almost directly behind him. He saw it shoot out over his head.

It was over, he knew, if Brantley was finished and the Orion vehicle had broken the Starfleet line behind him. They would be fighting two platforms in the front and at least one more behind them, one which was firing at nearly point-blank range.

Knowing he had nothing to lose, Kell turned over sharply and scanned for the platform. It was just meters away.

He aimed and had nearly fired when he heard Brantley yell, "Cease fire!" He stayed his finger, barely.

As the weapons platform approached, it took him a moment to process what he was looking at. He realized at once that the vehicle was not firing at the landing party. Rather, it was targeting the other platforms.

Kell also realized that it was not being piloted by an Orion, but by one of the primitives. He couldn't make out the face in the instant he had to look, but he recognized the humanoid's clothes. It was the first primitive they had seen, the one who had defeated the Orion pilot with a hand axe.

Then the platform passed over them, its cannons blazing.

The other vehicles didn't even get off a shot. The pilots seemed frozen. But their surprise didn't last long. The humanoid who was now just ahead of Kell and Kirk's position fired a series of lethal volleys that crashed through the Orions' shields.

One, then the other went up in a plume of orange fire. The sound of the nearby explosions was nearly deafening. Kell put his head down until the explosive blast passed over his head. Then he looked up.

Kirk was getting up, but keeping his phaser rifle pointed carefully at the ground.

As Kell got up, he saw Kirk look up at the primitive humanoid on the weapons platform, who had his back to the landing party.

In his peripheral vision, the Klingon saw the other primitives beginning to close in. He gripped his phaser rifle tightly. It was an old Klingon axiom that "The enemy of my enemy is my friend," but he did not know if these humanoids would feel the same way.

"I'm Captain James T. Kirk of the *Starship Enterprise*," the captain said.

The humanoid on the platform reacted to Kirk's voice by lowering the platform. He did it gently, as if he had piloted the craft before. Of course, that only made sense because he had just used it to blast two similar craft and their pilots to oblivion.

On the other hand, that realization didn't fit with the humanoid's hand-manufactured clothing. He was wearing a simple tan tunic and pants, made from a rough-hewn fabric. His shoes were some type of animal-hide leather, but also looked handmade and not manufactured.

When the platform was hovering barely off the

ground, the figure jumped to the ground and turned around.

At first, Kell rejected what his eyes told him as impossible. He took in the humanoid's face again, the dark skin, the bony ridges of the forehead.

Kell was looking into the face of a Klingon.

"I have learned about you," Klak said as Karel spoke to him in the Klingon commander's new quarters. In Karel's mind, he still had trouble thinking of Klak as *captain*.

Klak ate his evening *gagh* alone this time. He had not invited Karel to join him, for which the Klingon was grateful. He preferred to stand.

"I see you are a student of the fighting art *Mok'bara*, which explains your skill in hand fighting. I have also learned that you are a student of Kahless," Klak continued.

"I seek to follow in Kahless's path to honor and to victory," Karel said.

"Honor, like history, is decided by victors," Karel said.

Karel did not respond. He did not trust his ability to keep the distaste out of his voice. His father had taught him that honor, like truth, could not be twisted to serve a Klingon's ends.

"Tell me, what happened to Kahless?" Klak said.

"He was murdered," Karel said.

"As happens so often to Klingons of vision—too often," Klak said. "I do not wish to meet that fate. I have much glory I wish to bring to the Empire. And I would like you to help me."

"I serve the Empire," Karel said.

"And you wish vengeance against the Earthers," Klak said.

Karel nodded. "What would you like from me?" he asked.

"I want you to help me avoid Kahless's fate. I want you on the bridge with me the first duty cycle of each day," Klak said.

Karel guessed that Klak might ask him this. The new captain was worried about the loyalty of his bridge crew. At least in Koloth's case, Karel knew that worry was well founded.

To say no would be to make an enemy of Klak, but he was not prepared to give up his command of the disruptor room.

"I will serve you on the bridge," Karel said, "but I would like to then take the second duty cycle in the disruptor room with the Klingons I trained."

Klak was surprised by that, and it showed on his face. "You request a *second* duty cycle?"

"I believe I serve the Empire best in my disruptor room," Karel said.

"I offer you the bridge. You could learn much, and there is much *opportunity* there," Klak said. It was as close as Klak would come to offering Karel the job of bridge weapons officer. To take that position, he would have to challenge and kill Koloth, which would also take care of a serious problem for Klak.

Koloth had asked him if he sought favor over victory. Karel knew he did not. He sought victory and he sought revenge.

"I will serve you on the bridge. For now, I seek no other opportunities. I have much to learn first," Karel said.

Klak looked at him in frank amazement. He could

not believe that a Klingon would put duty above ambition.

"I am pleased to have a Klingon of your principles by my side," Klak said. "It is very important to the Empire that the ship accomplish its next mission against the Earthers."

Karel was suddenly very alert and he knew his interest showed on his face. Klak smiled and Karel noted again how unpleasant that smile was.

"The *D'k tahg* will be traveling into Federation space," he said.

"To engage the Earthers?" Karel asked.

"Not yet," Klak said. "We have to pick up cargo that will be vital in our coming war effort against the Federation. We have reports that the cargo may be in danger. Nothing must stop us and any Earthers who stand in our way must be destroyed."

So that was what Klak was offering Karel, a chance to see the beginning of the Empire's vengeance against the Earthers from the bridge. In return, he would have to help keep the new captain alive.

"I will see you on the bridge at the beginning of tomorrow's duty cycle," Karel said, as he turned to exit Klak's quarters.

Chapter Thirteen

THERE MUST BE *a simple explanation,* Kell thought. Co-incidence? Parallel development? The galaxy was teeming with races that looked more or less like humans. Why not another group that resembled Klingons?

Then the primitive humanoid, stepped forward, his eyes alert and said, "What is your purpose?"

It was a reasonable question. Not surprising under the circumstances, except that it was delivered in very clear Klingon.

Kirk did not understand, but Benitez stepped forward, and said, "He's speaking Klingon, sir."

Kirk was alert, but did not immediately raise his weapon. In fact, he raised a hand to calm Chief Brantley, who was raising his own rifle. Clearly, the captain understood that there was more going on here than there seemed.

The *Enterprise* had come to this planet suspecting a Klingon connection to the Orions. Yet this Klingon in primitive clothing had just saved their lives.

"You helped us, why?" the Klingon said. Karel tried to place the language. It was Klingon but with archaic usage and accents.

"What did he say, Mr. Benitez?" Kirk asked.

"I can't tell, sir. I don't speak Klingon very well. Ensign Anderson speaks it much better than me."

"Mr. Anderson?" Kirk asked.

Kell did not hesitate. "He asks us our purpose and wants to know why we helped them."

"Tell him we are here to stop the Orions and the damage they are doing here," Kirk said.

Kell translated. The Klingon listened carefully and said, "The enemy of my enemy is my friend," he said.

That was, of course, a Klingon proverb, and hearing it spoken in the archaic tongue gave Kell a chill. Something very strange was going on here.

Then the Klingon looked at him and asked, "Why do you fight the green skins?"

Kell translated for Kirk and then gave the captain's reply, "Because they work against our people and yours, and we don't like bullies."

The Klingon smiled at that, nodded, and said, "They shake the ground."

The Klingon might have been primitive, but he seemed to have a pretty good grasp of the situation. And he and his brothers had destroyed three Orion weapons platforms.

"Mr. Anderson, ask him if they are Klingons and if they serve the Klingon Empire," Kirk said.

The Klingon's response was that, yes, they were Klingons, but he did not recognize the term *Empire*.

The captain nodded when Kell relayed the response. Ensign Clark stepped forward and said, "Captain, xenoanthropologists have theorized for years that an ancient race seeded some planets with beings taken from other worlds. It explains why we encounter so many humanoid species. Perhaps the Klingons were seeded here somehow."

At Kirk's request, Kell asked the Klingon how long his people had been on this world. The Klingon looked at him questioningly and said, "Always. We have always been here."

In a flash of insight, Kell asked the Klingon if he had ever heard of Kahless. He had not. When Kell relayed this to the captain, Kirk said, "Then they arrived here more than fourteen hundred years ago."

Kell was surprised that Kirk knew of Kahless, but chalked it up to just one more surprise he had had in the company of humans. What Kirk said made sense. The Klingon's usage and speech reminded Kell of the Klingon tongue as it was spoken in Kahless's time, but it seemed even older.

The Klingon stepped forward and extended his hand. Kirk mirrored the gesture, and then the two men were grasping forearms. The Klingon said, "Gorath."

Kirk did not need a translation, "James T. Kirk," he said.

"We should not stay here. More green skins will come soon. They are fools but dangerous. You should come with us and we will see what we can accomplish together."

Kirk agreed, and one of the other primitive Klingons

jumped onto the remaining weapons platform to pilot it. Gorath led the way and Kirk followed.

Even after all he had seen, Kell had trouble believing that he was seeing Kirk walk in the company of a Klingon. The Federation was looking at war with the Empire, yet the fact that the primitive people they had come to protect had turned out to be of Klingon blood made no difference to the captain—or to the others for that matter.

Kell knew that if the situation were reversed and a Klingon force encountered a planet full of primitive humans within the Empire, the outcome would be quite different and very unpleasant for the humans.

This changed things for Kell, he knew. His mission to kill Captain Kirk would have to wait. Before he did that, he would first have to ensure that the captain succeeded in his mission to rid the planet of Orions.

More than one hundred thousand beings of Kell's own blood depended on Kirk, who was now walking alongside the primitive Klingon leader.

Humans, Kell thought, shaking his head.

But he found himself wondering what would develop out of the collaboration between these two men.

Lieutenant Commander Justman leaned over the auxiliary communications console, frantically looking for some evidence that what he had just seen had not been real.

"They must have jettisoned, but I can't find them on the scanners," the lieutenant at the science station said, an edge of panic in her voice.

That explanation made sense. The bridge design was modular so that bridges could be upgraded and replaced. The designers had also built them to act as lifeboats that could be jettisoned in an emergency.

If scanners didn't show anything, Justman would use his eyes. He worked the controls on the *Endeavor*'s viewer, looking for any sign of the jettisoned bridge. It wouldn't survive long in open space, particularly if the Klingons saw it first.

Then Justman saw something that stopped him cold. He held the image of the Yorkshire's damaged primary hull and magnified. Then he magnified again.

The hole left where the bridge should be looked like a gaping wound. And this wound was to the ship's core, both its brain and its heart.

Justman adjusted the angle again and he saw it clearly. Part of the helm/navigation console stood on the small piece of deck that was still there.

The bridge hadn't jettisoned. It could not be recovered.

It had been pulverized and blown into space. But that was impossible, because it meant the captain, First Officer Okuda, and the rest of the bridge crew were...gone.

And that couldn't be, because there were two Klingon cruisers just a few kilometers away and the captain had to get them out of this. Captain Rodriguez had to do what he always did. He had to win. The ship was depending on him. The people on Donatu V were depending on him.

The captain was too important to be...

He's gone, Justman thought. *They are all gone.*

It was unthinkable. It was impossible. But Justman knew it was also true and that the rest of the crew would follow them into oblivion unless the young officers in auxiliary control got hold of the situation. Even if they did, the *Yorkshire* might not survive.

Justman rejected that possibility. *Captain Rodriguez would be furious if we allowed that,* he thought.

"The transporter room can't get a fix on any of the bridge crew," the lieutenant at the science station said, his voice rising.

"The bridge is gone, they are all gone," Justman said, to the science officer and the room at large.

He saw the shock and dismay on the faces of the officers around him.

"We have to get control or we will lose the ship and Donatu V," he said, trying to muster some of the confidence he had heard just minutes ago in Captain Rodriguez's voice.

In his own mind he heard the roar of fear and the rising edge of panic, yet he forced them out of his voice.

"We still have a job to do and we have no choice but to succeed. We owe it to the captain," he said, again trying to give his voice a firmness and determination that he did not feel.

Fortunately, the officers around him apparently could not tell the difference, and he saw the rising tide of fear dissipate in the room. He needed to get them moving and quickly.

He turned to the communications officer, "Mr. Heller, tie all command lines and circuits into this room. Inform the rest of the ship that the bridge has been...damaged and we are routing command protocols here. Then find out who the ranking officer is and get them down here."

He turned to the engineering station, "Mr. Evans, you will have to coordinate damage control from here. Concentrate efforts on shields and weapons."

Then he turned to the young woman at the science station. "Ms. Parker, run continuous scans on the *Endeavor* and the Klingon battle cruisers. I want updates on the *Endeavor*'s survivors and I want to know what the Klingons are doing every second."

"Sir," Acting Communications Officer Heller said, "the Klingons are hailing us."

"Where's the ranking officer? Someone has to tell them that they are in command," Justman barked.

"Sir, *you* are the ranking officer," Heller said.

It was another impossibility. He could not be the ranking officer when there was the captain...or lieutenant commander...

Then Justman realized that all the people he looked to in tense or dangerous situations were dead.

"Is it the lead ship hailing?" Justman said.

"Yes," came the communications officer's reply.

"Status of the Klingon vessel?" he asked.

The science officer took a moment and then said, "Their shields are almost gone down and warp engines are...experiencing power fluctuations."

Justman's hands flew over his own console and he saw that the *Yorkshire*'s weapons were at full power and shields were at better than sixty percent and climbing.

The ship was nearly fully functional, if you discounted the fact that it had lost its heart, soul, and mind moments ago.

Justman took a moment to study the viewscreen, which now showed the lead Klingon cruiser standing behind the *Endeavor*. Clearly, the Klingon commander wanted to make it harder for the *Yorkshire* to fire and also wanted to use its own proximity to the ship as a threat.

Justman decided he was done being threatened.

"Put the Klingon on the main viewer," he said.

A moment later, the Klingon commander Maarcs's face appeared onscreen.

"This is Lieutenant Commander Robert H. Justman, acting commander of the *United Space Ship Yorkshire*."

The Klingon smiled an unpleasant smile. "You can still see your captain, you know, but you will have to carefully calibrate your sensors. He is in very small pieces."

That hurt, but Justman would be dammed if he let the Klingon see it.

"How is your warp reactor?" Justman said. "It is unfortunate that when you finally retreat you will have to do it at sublight speeds."

Justman saw that he had scored a direct psychological hit. The Klingon roared in anger. The lieutenant commander decided to press his advantage, perhaps the only one he would see today. "Is that why you cower behind the *Endeavor?* Are you trying to postpone your humiliation?" Justman said.

Watching the Klingon's eyes bulge and the veins in his neck throb, he wondered if it was possible for Klingons to literally burst with rage.

"Surrender now," Justman said.

"You insolent Earther fool!" the Klingon said when he was finally able to speak. "I will destroy this worthless hulk in front of me, then I will take your ship. I offered your captain a quick death, but you and your crew will now die slowly."

The Klingon obviously broke the connection, because the face was replaced by the view of the *Endeavor* and the Klingon cruisers.

For a moment, Justman could feel the eyes of the auxiliary-control crew on him. They were looking to him, hoping he had a plan, a plan beyond taunting the Klingon commander into a rage.

He was sorry that he would disappoint them.

Chapter Fourteen

"YOU ARE FROM space as well?" Gorath asked.

Kell translated. He could see that Kirk and the others were as surprised as he was, both by Gorath's understanding of space travel and his casual acceptance of it.

"Yes, we are," Kirk replied.

Gorath had brought the landing party to his small village a few kilometers away from the place where they had fought the Orions. They were sitting on wooden stools in the center of the village. Kirk and Gorath were facing each other, with Kell sitting next to the captain to translate. Whatever his title, Gorath was clearly the leader of this community.

Chief Brantley and the others were nearby, as were a small group of Gorath's men. Kell guessed they were the same Klingons who had accompanied the Klingon on the hunt for the Orion vehicle, which, Kell noted, had disappeared into the village somewhere.

The village reminded Kell of images and re-creations he had seen of ancient Klingon life. It had simple but well-constructed wooden structures. They had obviously been built with hand tools, but were more refined than simple log structures.

The smaller buildings were dwellings, he guessed. Larger buildings must have served some community purpose. Kell noted that the Klingons were working with metal tools, so they had learned to find and manipulate iron and other ores.

The overall impression the village gave was one of order. It was also peaceful. Children played, craftsmen worked, and hunters brought in prey. Their lives continued with confidence, despite the fact that the shadow of destruction at the hands of the Orions loomed over them.

Kell felt as if he were looking through time at a glimpse of his own honored ancestors. He felt the pull to preserve this place and these people and a flash of rage at the Orions who would destroy them so carelessly.

"We belong to a Federation of worlds in the larger galaxy that has banded together for mutual enrichment and protection," Kirk explained.

"Are there many dangerous people like the green skins?" Gorath asked.

"We have found most peoples to be open to friendship, but, yes, there are dangerous races as well," Kirk said. The captain thought for a moment and continued. "We believed the Orions were working for another race who seek to harm us. We thought the Orions were taking crystals from the earth to help power ships and weapons."

Gorath nodded. "Then we truly have a common enemy," he said.

"True," Kirk said. "We believed this enemy the Orions served to be of your blood, but that seems unlikely now."

It was true. The Empire would not be behind this destructive mining on a planet full of Klingons. But the question remained, Who was behind it? He wondered what Benitez would make of the situation. No doubt his roommate would have a theory.

"These people of our blood, these fellow Klingons who travel the stars, how did they get there?" Gorath asked.

Kirk asked Kell to explain the theory that an ancient powerful race seeded the Klingons who now lived on this world.

Gorath listened carefully and with interest. "How do you know for certain that we are the seed? Perhaps we are the source and these Klingons who travel space are our seed?"

Like Kell, the captain was surprised by the idea, but could not completely discount it. "We do not know for certain," he said.

Parrish approached with her tricorder out.

"Report," Kirk asked.

"Sir, to do a proper geological survey, we would need the ship's sensors and some more equipment on the ground," she said.

"Best guess, Ensign," Kirk said.

"I think this planet and these people are in big trouble, Captain," she said.

As if to punctuate her words, the ground began to

shake. It was not as powerful as the earthquake they had felt when they arrived, but it was enough to make the point.

"The late stages of deep-core mining creates massive earthquakes, tremendous volcanic activity, tidal waves, and even polar shifts. They do not have long, sir," Parrish said.

Kirk dismissed Parrish and asked Kell to translate. Gorath seemed concerned but not surprised.

"We could see they were doing damage, but enough to destroy the world..." Gorath said.

"We are here to protect you," Kirk said with confidence.

Gorath shook his head. "We welcome help, but we do not need protection. We do our own fighting," he said, finally.

"I cannot allow you and your people to pit themselves against the Orions and their weapons," Kirk said.

Gorath smiled. "We do not ask permission, Captain. The *Orions* are our problem and I have a plan for dealing with them, though we will have to move more quickly then I intended. I wished to collect more tribute from the green skins."

"Tribute?" Kirk asked Kell.

"I do not know what he means, Captain," Kell said.

Kirk smiled. "We are your guests. We will offer you whatever help we can."

Just then, the ground shook beneath them. Kell quickly realized that it was not another earthquake when he heard the nearly simultaneous explosion. He turned to see a bright orange mushroom rise in the distance.

Kell immediately saw that it came from roughly the place where they had left the shuttle.

The captain was on his feet immediately.

"That was the shuttle, sir," Parrish said, checking her tricorder.

Kell thought he heard the captain mutter some nonregulation language under his breath and he understood why.

The mission just became exponentially more dangerous and more difficult. The Orions knew they were here.

"Sir, something happened on the surface," Junior Science Officer Stern said from the science station. "An explosion."

Spock was out of the command seat immediately and was at the science station in a moment. The young lieutenant stepped aside and Spock looked into the computer viewer.

He could see Mr. Scott's work to increase power and sensitivity to track the shuttle. He backed the readings up and found the shuttle clearly on the surface. Then he traced the sensor records forward, saw a power spike that could only be an explosion, and then saw the shuttle's signal disappear.

"What is it, Spock," McCoy asked from behind him.

"The shuttle has been destroyed," Spock said.

He saw the surprise register on the doctor's face and heard the sharp intake of breath of the rest of the bridge crew. Their concern over something they could not change would hamper efficiency. He had to do something to reduce their anxiety.

"I have no reason to believe the landing party was on board. In fact, it is unlikely, given the fact that the shuttle had landed and was in standby mode at the time," he said.

"How will the captain call for help without the shuttle's transmitter?" McCoy asked.

"Lieutenant Uhura, have you had any success?" Spock asked.

The communications officer turned around and said, "I'm not getting anything on the landing party's communications channels. However, I am getting some chatter now on the Orion frequencies."

Uhura listened carefully for a moment, then said, "They are looking for someone...Starfleet. They have put out an alert."

"Sp—" McCoy began.

Spock stopped him with a raised hand. "Mr. Sulu, full impulse to the planet. Lieutenant Uhura, order a yellow alert and have Lieutenant Commander Giotto prepare a team to beam down to the surface."

Spock took the command seat. He did a quick estimation of the time required to the planet. At full impulse, the *Enterprise* would reach the world in seventeen point four six seven minutes.

"If they found the shuttle then the captain won't have much time, if they are still all right," Dr. McCoy said.

The doctor was right, seventeen minutes might be too long.

"Lieutenant Uhura, hail the Orion installation. Tell them the *Enterprise* is on its way to take control of their illegal operation. They are to abandon all mining activities as well as any other aggressive activities."

"Think that will convince them to give themselves up," McCoy said. The smile on the doctor's face told Spock that the human was not asking the question in a literal sense. It was difficult to tell with humans, the Vulcan had learned.

"No," Spock replied. "But it will give them something to worry about besides the landing party."

Karel entered Klak's quarters. The Klingon nodded to Karel and put on his *d'k tahg* blade. Before he could finish, the viewer on his desk flashed.

"Wait," the commander said to him, and hit the switch on his viewer.

Karel watched as a Klingon wearing the uniform of a high commander appeared on the screen.

"Captain Klak," the Klingon said. "I have new orders for you. A federation starship is on its way to the installation. They will be there in minutes."

"We are still hours away, even at maximum warp," Klak said.

"But you are not hours away from the border between Klingon and Federation space. Cross it now and make sure the Earthers see you," the high commander said.

Klak looked concerned, "But I thought stealth..." he said.

"Stealth is the last thing we want now. Make sure the Earthers see you with their sensor probes. Draw that starship away," the high commander said. "Then wait for more orders."

"I serve the Empire," Klak said as the high commander broke the connection.

"You may get to pay the Earthers back sooner than you thought, Senior Weapons Officer Karel," the commander said.

Karel hoped that was true.

Yet he was troubled by Klak's tone. He did not hear confidence in the Klingon's voice. Klak had shown surprise when he learned that the *D'k tahg* would not be sneaking into Federation space.

Karel preferred the notion of the ship announcing itself, making its entrance a challenge that would put the Earthers on notice.

Yet he heard something else in Klak's voice. Was it caution, or cowardice?

Chapter Fifteen

"THE SECOND KLINGON CRUISER is moving into position," Acting Science Officer Parker said.

Justman nodded. The lead ship was reluctant to engage them. The damage to their nacelle was great and their starboard shield was probably still down, which explained why the Klingon captain was keeping the starboard side of his ship behind the *Endeavor*'s primary hull.

"Helm, pull away from the *Endeavor.* Let's see if we can put some distance between us and the lead ship. Maybe they will stay out of the battle for a while."

They would probably stay out as long as the *Endeavor* remained intact and a threat. Then Justman had no doubt the Klingon commander would take pleasure in finishing them. Well, he did not intend to give them a chance.

"Sir, there's something happening on the *Endeavor.* A power surge," the acting science officer said.

"Is the Klingon cruiser firing on them?" Justman asked.

"No, sir. I think the ship is powering up phasers," she said.

"Put the *Endeavor* on screen and magnify," Justman said. He kept a careful eye on the second Klingon cruiser with his tactical sensors. It was powering weapons itself.

Justman spared a look at the main viewer and saw the impossible happen before his eyes. The crippled primary hull of the *Endeavor* shot out a single beam of red energy, directly into the damaged and nearly unprotected starboard side of the lead Klingon cruiser.

"What's happening?" the science officer said.

"Captain Shannon is happening," Justman said as he watched the Klingon cruiser shudder under the assault.

The phaser beam stopped and Justman watched as the cruiser turned to pull away. That must have been what Captain Shannon was waiting for, because another beam lanced out, striking the Klingon ship square in the damaged nacelle.

Though it was only a single phaser bank firing, the Klingon's shield failed in a flash of light. Then the beam cut right into the hull of the ship.

The continuous beam cut through and then severed the nacelle. Then moved up to the main hull, cutting into the very heart of the ship.

The Klingon vessel tried to use maneuvering thrusters to move out of the way. It actually put a few hundred meters' more distance between it and the *Endeavor*. Justman wondered why the Klingons didn't use impulse engines to escape.

Then he understood when he saw the phasers cut closer and closer to the rear of the ship, where the impulse engine system was housed. The system must have been blown, he realized. Yet the Klingons put another perhaps thousand meters between it and the *Endeavor.*

It was not nearly enough. The phaser tracked the ship and continued its lethal path. Justman imagined systems overloading and bulkheads crumbling. He could see debris being sucked out through multiple hull breaches.

The Klingon ship was dying and it pained Justman to see it. He imagined that the *Endeavor* must have also sustained terrible damage before Captain Shannon had given the order to separate the main hull.

That was a desperate act of a captain who was trying to save his crew even as he lost his ship. The primary hull could function as an excellent lifeboat, even at minimal power. But it was never supposed to be taken into battle.

Somehow, Captain Shannon had brought the remains of the *Endeavor* back into the battle. And he had done it while a Klingon boarding party controlled most of the crippled ship.

In the end, Justman couldn't tell whether the phaser struck the impulse engines directly or the torpedo room that served the rear torpedo shaft. Whatever the phaser hit last, it caused the Klingon cruiser to explode in a brilliant flash of light and energy that traveled through subspace and rocked the *Yorkshire.*

It shook the even closer *Endeavor* much harder.

"I'm showing no power in the *Endeavor,*" Lieutenant Parker said.

Justman was determined to see that Captain Shannon and his crew's incredible effort was not wasted.

"Helm, I want a near-miss course on the remaining Klingon vessel," he said, knowing he had to hit the

Klingon vessel while it was still reeling from the loss of its lead ship.

For the first time since he realized the captain and the bridge crew were gone, Justman thought they might actually have a chance.

"They want to come along?" Benitez asked.

"Is the captain going to allow it?" Clark asked.

"The leader, Gorath...insisted. Apparently, they have been planning some kind of raid on the installation for some time," Kell said. He spared a glance toward Gorath and about a dozen other Klingons as they conferred outside one of the larger buildings, while Captain Kirk and Section Chief Brantley spoke nearby.

"We can't be worrying about them when we go in," Ensign Sobel said.

"They did capture an Orion weapons platform with rocks and an axe," Kell said. "In any case, the point is settled. We have their help, or they have ours, depending on how you look at it."

The others nodded, apparently satisfied. That alone amazed Kell. The humans were not questioning whether or not they would help the *Klingon* primitives. Their only concern was whether or not those primitives would be a help or hindrance.

The humans around him did not do this after wrestling with their principles; they did it as a matter of course—as if there were no other course.

Kell knew that if the Klingon Empire won the coming fight, they would try to smash the surviving humans' spirits. He doubted that would be even possible, even if the humans were defeated. And even if it were possible, the loss of such strength of purpose would be a great loss to the galaxy.

Suddenly, Kell heard a whoop in the distance. It was followed by another, then another, each closer than the last.

Suddenly, the village was alive with movement, with Klingons running back and forth. But the movement was not frantic, instead it was filled with purpose.

Something was happening.

Kell and the squad ran toward Kirk and Brantley's position and arrived just as Gorath did.

"It begins. The green skins are coming," Gorath said, and Kell translated.

"Captain, I don't show anything," Parrish said, studying her tricorder.

Kirk didn't hesitate. "Check your weapons," he ordered as he checked his own phaser rifle.

"Come," Gorath said, motioning for the squad to follow.

Gorath was met by about twenty other Klingons, both males and females, who looked to him intently. Obviously waiting for instructions.

The Klingon leader gave a nod and his Klingons went to work. They surrounded the wooden structure and a moment later its walls fell away. The building had obviously been a shell. Now only its roof was standing, supported by four large posts.

"Orion tribute," Gorath said, pointing to the contents of the building.

It was tribute indeed, and far superior to rocks and an axe.

Kell took a quick inventory. There were three Orion

weapons platforms that looked to be completely intact. There were also two tables full of Orion weapons, both rifles and sidearm. Kell had seen firsthand how deadly those weapons could be in the hands of even inept Orions.

Side by side with the powerful energy weapons were weapons that Kell recognized: Klingon *mek'leths,* precursors to the *bat'leth,* the honored blade first forged by the hand of Kahless himself.

The Klingons descended on the tables and suddenly the Orion weapons were in the hands of Klingon warriors, warriors who had brought down a shielded and armored weapons platform with little more than their bare hands.

Seeing the landing party's naked astonishment, Gorath smiled and said, "One does not fight fire with grass."

Kirk raised an eyebrow and said, "Apparently not."

Gorath offered Kirk a *mek'leth.* Without hesitation, the captain accepted it and strapped it on. Then the rest of the landing party accepted the offered blades, and Kell took his own. He felt his blood burn when he touched the metal handle with one hand and the blade with the other, staring at the weapon in awe.

He quickly tied the leather belt that held the blade around his waist and saw that the other officers were doing the same.

The captain approached one of the weapons platforms and said, "I will give one of them a try. Who else has a combat flight rating?"

Chief Brantley stepped forward, but Gorath stayed him with a polite but firm hand on the shoulder.

The Klingon leader did not understand the captain's words, but he obviously understood the human's intention. Gorath leaped onto one platform and signaled two other Klingons, a male and a female, who did the same on the other two platforms.

With a quick series of movements that spoke of long practice, the three Klingons powered up the platforms and maneuvered them outside. Once there, they brought the platforms up to about two meters above the ground.

Gorath looked down on the assembled Klingons and the landing party and said, "Let them come." Then he quickly gave instructions to his warriors.

"Captain, he is telling them to take their positions and suggests we do the same. They will be taking cover on either side of the center or the village. He asks us to take this side," Kell said, pointing to a line of trees nearby.

"Tell him we will," Kirk said.

The Klingons quickly redistributed themselves, with twelve spread out on one side of the village behind the dwellings and five more accompanying the eight members of the landing party to the line of trees.

As they took position, Benitez stayed close beside him. The others did the same, staying close to their partners.

He saw Parrish and Ensign Sobel take cover behind one of the trees. Before she disappeared from view, Parrish smiled at him, a smile that he returned. Whatever happened, he hoped he had time to finish things properly with her.

Kell noticed that the village was extremely quiet. He also realized that it was completely deserted, except for the warriors who would now defend it. Kell was proud to be among them.

He glanced at Benitez, who smiled at him. Kell returned the smile, and then it began.

Five warriors came running toward the center of town

from the distant woods. As Gorath had been when they first saw him, the Klingons were dodging, finding cover where they could, making themselves difficult targets.

Then Kell saw what was chasing them. Four weapons platforms, piloted by the now familiar figure of tall Orions wearing armored suits.

The platforms tried to track the Klingons, but the nimble and fast warriors managed to avoid the deadly energy blasts. As the Klingons led the Orions toward the center of town, Kell realized that they were using the pincer formation again.

Except this time, the Klingons on each side of the pincer were carrying phaser rifles and Orion energy weapons. And even if the Orions survived the strikes from each side, the Klingon was sure that three weapons platforms piloted by Klingons were waiting for them at the apex of the formation.

Suddenly, a blast from one of the vehicles hit one of the warriors, who disappeared in a flash of light and energy.

To Kell it seemed both impossible and supremely unjust that the cowardly Orion could end the valiant primitive Klingon's life. The others continued, drawing the platforms closer and closer to the pincer's snare. Then, when they were perhaps ten meters from the position of the outermost Klingons, Gorath gave a Klingon war cry—the same cry that had rung out on countless battlefields in Klingon history.

Kell added his voice to the cry and so did, he noticed, Benitez and the other security officers nearby.

A weapon fired from nearby, one of the captured Orion weapons now in the hands of a Klingon.

"Fire!" he heard Kirk's voice shout. And then the

phaser rifle in his hand came alive with deadly power. He picked his first target and was pleased to see its shield flare purple under the assault.

Suddenly, Kell was filled with pride as he watched the Klingons begin firing. He felt that he was fighting beside his honored ancient ancestors, Klingons who fought bravely to protect their homes and families, Klingons who fought a just battle and fought it well.

These Orions were not as foolish as the others he had seen. Once they realized they were under fire, they accelerated their vehicles, quickly shooting in front of Kell's position. The Klingon tracked his target and was pleased to see its shield flare and flicker, already showing signs that it would fail soon.

Gorath's and the other two weapons platforms appeared on Kell's far left—the apex of the pincer. They shot forward to meet the four Orion platforms.

Seeing the other platforms, the Orion pilots did not even slow down. Kell imagined that their first thought was that they had found salvation and were being joined in battle by more of their brothers.

Even when Gorath and his two warriors opened fire, the Orions continued forward, obviously not yet comprehending their true danger.

When the two groups of armored vehicles were less than one hundred meters apart, the two Orion pilots on the outside of the formation peeled away. The two in the middle did not, and they stayed their course as Gorath and the others shot toward them, cannons blazing.

To their credit, each Orion pilot managed to get off a single shot before the Klingons were upon them, but neither shot found a target.

Finally, at nearly point-blank range, Gorath and his warriors let loose with fierce barrages of energy blasts.

They did not miss.

The two Orion platforms in the center exploded in brilliant balls of fire, which Gorath and his Klingons flew through victoriously.

By now, the pilots of the two outer platforms had decided to rejoin the battle. They had gained altitude to avoid the fire from the ground. Now they were aiming below and shooting at Gorath and his two "wingmen" as they cleared the explosions.

Instantly alert, Gorath and the two other Klingon pilots banked hard in a violent maneuver that turned them directly into the direction of the fire.

Seeing the Klingons come speeding toward them and ignore the fire that came their way, the Orions reconsidered and tried to pull away. It was a clumsy maneuver, the kind made by cowardly fools who were used to prey that did not fight back.

The Klingons, on the other hand, were hunters whose reflexes and instincts had been honed through countless lifetimes. The Klingons chased the Orions, who were now trying openly to flee. Gorath followed one of the vehicles, while the other two Klingons followed the other.

It was over in a matter of seconds.

The warriors around them gave a cheer at seeing the last two platforms explode, and Kell smiled his own satisfaction.

"Do you get the feeling that we are the ones getting in the way?" Benitez said, smiling.

Before Kell could agree, Parrish's voice called out. "I

show some movement on the ground. And something else in the air...something big."

Kell looked into the distance and saw movement. Ground forces, he saw, perhaps sixty of them.

Then he saw something in the air above them. It was big, perhaps five or six times the size of the Orion platforms. Still a platform, it had a single pilot near the front and three gunners on each side, each manning a cannon at least the size of the ones on the other platforms.

It was a familiar strategy. Send in the light attack craft, followed by heavier equipment and ground forces. Kell called on his blood for strength. It was a very effective battle plan, especially if the attacking force had greater numbers.

And the Orions now outnumbered the Klingon and Starfleet personnel at least three to one.

"Approaching Federation space," Commander Koloth said from his weapons station on the bridge.

"Have you plotted the Federation's sensor outposts?" Klak asked.

Karel stood at the new captain's right, while the other guard, a large Klingon named Ranc, stood on his left. Ranc was the same one who had betrayed and helped murder Captain Kran.

Karel wondered if Klak had considered the possibility that if Ranc could betray the captain, whom he was honor-bound to protect, he might also betray Klak.

Suddenly, Karel was certain that Klak had not considered it. In his arrogance, Klak no doubt thought that he commanded some greater loyalty than Kran had. In truth, Karel could see that Ranc was honorless and serving the lesser master named Klak would not make him any less so.

"I have all of the sensor outposts on my screen," Koloth said.

"Feed coordinates of the closest one to the helm," Klak said.

"Done," Koloth replied.

"Helm, take us as close as you can to the senor array," Klak said.

All of the Klingons on the bridge gasped in surprise, except for Karel, who knew this was coming.

"You do not want me to avoid the drones?" the helmsman asked.

"Follow my order!" Klak shouted. "I will not be questioned by cowards who fear the Federation weaklings."

The helmsmen manipulated his controls and said, "It is done."

Karel could see Klak sit back, a satisfied expression on his face. Karel shook his head at Klak's tactics. The commander had expressed the same thought, when he received his own orders, and Karel thought he had seen fear in the Klingon's eyes then.

Now he was berating an officer for expressing what the entire bridge crew was thinking. And instead of telling his subordinates the purpose of their mission, Klak was humiliating one and sowing doubt in minds of the others.

Kell's blood burned at the thought of serving and protecting such a Klingon.

Chapter Sixteen

"Now, HELM," Justman said, and he felt the *Yorkshire* shudder under his feet as it shot toward the Klingon cruiser.

He confirmed that the phasers were charged and the photon torpedoes armed. With luck they would execute the maneuver and fire weapons before the Klingons could respond.

He fired one torpedo, then another, before he saw that though they were certainly due some luck, the Klingons would not be granting any just yet.

His warning light told him that the Klingon cruiser had a weapons lock on the *Yorkshire*. Justman ignored it and targeted the phasers.

He saw the torpedoes hit the Klingon cruiser's shields directly and fired the phasers an instant before he felt the impact of the Klingon torpedo on the *Yorkshire*. Ignoring the alarms on his weapons console, Justman fired and fired again.

He watched on his forward tactical display as the Klingon cruiser grew to fill it. Just before it looked like the vessels would collide, he saw open space and knew they were past the cruiser.

The wise thing to do would be to retreat, assess damage, and plan the next phase of the battle, but Justman rejected the conventional wisdom. He was an inexperienced commander, commanding a heavily damaged ship run by a group of brave but green lieutenants. And he was fighting an aggressive foe who had no doubt years of experience in combat situations.

Justman sensed that if he did not end the battle quickly, the longer it drew out the greater the chance that one of the Klingon ships' many advantages would tip the battle in their favor.

Ignoring the damage reports and alerts on his own console, Justman called out, "Helm, turn us around and bring us in close again."

As Justman again felt the pull of high-speed impulse maneuvers, his hands raced across his console. He tried to make sense out of the sensor data the science officer was feeding him on the status of the Klingon ship.

The *Endeavor* and the *Yorkshire* had hit them hard, but the Klingon's shields were holding up well—better than the *Yorkshire*'s own, a look at the monitor told him.

The ship wouldn't take many more torpedo hits. When the *Yorkshire* was properly oriented for another run on the Klingon cruiser, he let loose a volley of four torpedoes and detonated them about midway between the two ships.

The blast and the radiation would render the Klingon

vessel's targeting systems ineffective. Unfortunately, it would do the same for the *Yorkshire*'s systems. The difference was that Justman knew it was coming and was prepared to fire the phasers manually.

Fractions of a second later, the *Yorkshire* was once again nearly on top of the cruiser. Justman fired phasers, targeting by eye. He didn't try to get fancy and look for weaknesses in the shields. Instead, he aimed for the largest target he could find: the rear, engineering section of the ship.

He got off four blasts before the *Yorkshire* overshot the cruiser. He thought all of them were hits but couldn't be sure and he dared not take an instant to check the sensor data.

Instead he was shouting out an order and checking his torpedo status. "Helm, maintain course and speed, but turn us to face them," he shouted.

The helmsman replied with an "Aye," and Justman could imagine the *Yorkshire* shooting away from the Klingon ship, but turning as it did to face its enemy.

As soon as the readout told him they were properly oriented he let loose with a volley of torpedoes. One. Then another. Then another. Then another, as he watched the Klingon cruiser on his screen recede.

He waited for the reload indicator and fired two more.

Only then did he spare a glance at his readouts. As he suspected, the Klingon ship had not been able to fire a shot at them. And they were making no move to pursue.

"Ms. Parker, status of the Klingon ship?" he called out.

There was an edge in her voice as she said. "Sir, their shields are down...I'm showing massive overloads, energy spiking off the charts..."

Justman glanced at the main viewer in time to see the Klingon cruiser explode in a brilliant flash on the screen.

He had to close his eyes for a moment because the flare was so bright. When he opened them again the flare of the explosion seemed to linger; then it extinguished itself, disappearing as quickly as it had appeared.

Then the subspace shock wave hit—not as powerful this time, since the distance from the exploding cruiser was greater this time.

The *Yorkshire* was rocked for a moment; then the moment passed and there were a few seconds of silence as the auxiliary-control crew digested what they had just witnessed.

Then the chatter from the communications station broke the silence as damage reports came from all over the ship.

"Sir," the communications officer said. "We're being hailed by the planet...and from the...*Endeavor.*"

"Tell Donatu V to wait. Put the *Endeavor* on," Justman said.

"I only have audio, sir," the lieutenant at communications said.

Then a male voice said, *"Yorkshire,* this is the *Endeavor.*" The channel was remarkably clear and the voice surprisingly calm, as if it were a routine message.

"This is the *Yorkshire.* Lieutenant Commander Robert H. Justman, acting commander, here," he said.

"This is Ensign Michael Fuller," the voice said. "It's good to hear your voice. We were able to monitor some of the battle from here. Is it over?"

"The two Klingon cruisers are neutralized, thanks to

your efforts over there. Those phasers came at just the right time. Is Captain Shannon with you?" Justman said.

There was a pause on the other side, then, "No, Captain Shannon didn't make it, but we have him to thank for the phasers."

"Understood. I'm sorry about your losses. How many of you are there? And are there any Klingons on board?"

"The Klingons have been...neutralized. There are just five of us," he said.

"Stay together, we will pick you up shortly. I look forward to shaking your hand, Mr. Fuller."

"And I yours, sir. Fuller out."

"Helm, bring us alongside the *Endeavor*. Mr. Heller, tell the transporter room to stand by," Justman said.

Then for the first time since he arrived at auxiliary control, Lieutenant Commander Justman sat. He let himself fall into the chair next to his weapons console.

He felt the beginnings of grief well up in his throat and forced it back down. He had no time for that indulgence and he doubted that he would be able to function when it hit him with its full force.

"Sir, I am getting another hail," the communications officer said.

Justman almost told him to tell the party on Donatu V to wait when Lieutenant Heller finished with. "It's from a Klingon cruiser."

Immediately alert, Justman was on his feet without realizing that he had stood up. He turned to the science station. "Sensors, Ms. Parker?"

"It is one of three Klingon ships, sir," Parker said.

"How much time do we have?" Justman said.

"A little less than one hour, sir," she replied. Then

she checked her viewer and looked up. "Sir, it's going to be at least three hours until the Starfleet vessels get here."

Justman went back to his console. Shields were at thirty percent. In an hour, engineering might be able to get them back to fifty or even sixty percent. Weapons were functioning but that was thin comfort.

He tied his tactical display into the science station's sensors. Three heavily armed, fully functional Klingon battle cruisers were on their way.

Justman realized that the Battle of Donatu V was far from over.

He checked the chronometer on his console. Actually, not that far. The Klingons would arrive in fifty-seven minutes.

Not long after that, he feared, the battle would be over for good.

"Put the Klingons on the screen," Justman heard himself say.

A moment later a Klingon face dominated the auxiliary-control main viewer. "Federation ship, abandon the Donatu system or be destroyed," the Klingon said.

"You are in violation of Federation space. Return to Klingon space immediately or face dire consequences," Justman said. It was an empty threat, he knew, but it felt good to make it.

The Klingon on screen laughed. "We have monitored your battle from here. You are alone, with your only support hours away. Stay and you will pay for your crimes against the Klingon Empire. Run and we will catch you and then you will pay. Either way, Earther, you all die—today."

Justman's peripheral vision told him the entire auxiliary control crew was looking at him—looking *to* him.

They were looking to him for strength, the way he had looked to Captain Rodriguez. The difference was that the captain was a great man. At the moment, Justman felt like a thin shadow, but the crew looked at him with respect just the same.

He said a quick prayer to Captain Rodriguez wherever he was asking for strength, and when his mouth opened he was surprised to hear that his voice was calm, steady.

"Klingon commander," Justman said. "This ship does not run from any threat. If you have any doubt about that check your scanners. You will find the Klingon fleet short two battle cruisers. Continue on your current course at your own peril."

Then he turned to the communications officer and said, "Mr. Heller, close channel."

When the scene on the viewer changed back to space, it showed the primary hull of the *Endeavor.*

"Is the transporter room ready, Mr. Heller?" he said.

"Yes, sir," the lieutenant said.

"Then beam the survivors on board," Justman said.

Kell watched as Gorath and his two fellow Klingon pilots did not hesitate. They immediately accelerated toward the large Orion platform, even as the Orions fired their first shots at the smaller vehicles.

As he watched the Klingons race across the sky, he saw Gorath take center position and the other two Klingons each take a flank. Kell immediately saw why.

The Orion platform had a weakness that Gorath must have seen immediately. Each of the guns was mounted on the side. The platform had no forward gun. It was well designed for causing maximum damage to ground forces. But it was not meant for air combat. The gunners on the side would be able to shoot effectively only at targets that were considerate enough to fly alongside it.

Obviously, the primitive Klingons did not intend to be considerate.

Gorath and the others kept their formation tight and barreled straight for the platform. The pilot reacted slowly to the new development and did not think to turn his craft until it was too late to do any good.

Gorath and the others fired their cannons from close range, and each Klingon made at least three solid hits on the larger ship's shields before overshooting it. The shields glowed red when they were hit, telling Kell that the larger ship had a much more powerful shield than the smaller platforms.

With the Orion platform turned, the gunners on one side were able to shoot at the craft from behind as they sped away. However, the Klingons were executing aggressive evasive maneuvers that Kell suspected pushed the design limits of the Orion vehicles.

The Orion gunners didn't even come close.

By now the Orion ground forces were closing in and Kell had to turn his attention back to the battle at hand. He had to trust that Gorath and his brothers would take care of the Orion battle platform. Otherwise, the Klingons on the ground and the landing party would not survive—even if they managed to somehow survive the Orions now approaching them.

Karel counted about sixty.

"Do you think the Orions even know what the term 'fair fight' means?" Benitez said.

"Apparently not," Kell said.

The Orions stopped near the entrance of the village. Two of them in the lead conferred for a few seconds, and the teams split into two forces of about thirty. Each of the two teams took one side of the village and moved forward slowly.

The Orions obviously had sensors. Kell saw that they would not be running through the center of the village and the center of the pincer, where they would be in the crossfire.

Instead, the Orions sought cover of their own and opened fire on the defensive forces on either side. The primitive Klingons returned the fire, as did Kell and the rest of the landing party, but he immediately saw the problem when the first Klingon fell to Orion fire.

Once again, the Orions outnumbered the defenders. In addition, their armor gave them limited protection from phaser fire and energy beams from the stolen Orion weapons. It was not enough to protect them from a direct hit, but a glancing blow that would kill or at least incapacitate an unprotected Klingon or human would be absorbed by the armor.

It was simple math. Even if the defenders fought bravely and much better than the Orions, attrition would eventually give the battle to the attackers.

Seconds in, Kell could see the end of the battle in his mind. That end might be glorious, but it would be final and result in the failure of the mission. And then the mining would continue and an entire planet full of Klingons would be lost.

Kirk obviously saw the same thing and appeared next to Kell. "Mr. Anderson, we can't fight them on these terms. We have to get in close, so close that they won't be able to use their weapons without risking hitting each other. Tell the Klingons we need to move closer, in between them if we can, and use the blades," the captain said, patting his *mek'leth*.

It was dangerous, but Kell knew Kirk was right. They would at least have a chance. Kell shouted the instructions, and the Klingons immediately abandoned their cover and started moving, dodging and feinting, giving their battle cry as they went.

The landing party had to hurry to keep up. Kell spared a glance at the Klingons on the other side and saw they were following suit. He also caught a quick glimpse of the battle in the air.

In the instant he looked, he saw one of the Klingon-piloted weapons platforms hurtling down and out of control. He had to look forward before it hit, but the explosion that followed seconds later told him what he needed to know.

Kell hoped it was not a bad omen for the battle as he ran. He kept Benitez in his peripheral vision and fired as he charged the Orion line.

He took care with his aim. The Klingons in the lead were already practically on top of the Orions, who were recoiling. Then the enemies were too close together for Kell to fire safely. He noted that the officers around him also held their fire.

Reaching for his hip, Kell drew the *mek'leth*. He had not held one in years, since his last *targ* hunt with his brother. He remembered the hunt; it was just before

Karel had taken his post with the Klingon Defense Force.

With a pang, Kell realized that it was the last *targ* hunt he would ever have with his brother. Yet, even as that thought filled him, he realized that he and the others had to succeed here today. And not only that, but he must survive to somehow report the Orions' treachery to Klingon command.

The Orions had to pay for what they were doing on this world. He had faith in the humans to fight and win against difficult odds. But he knew they would never take the kind of revenge that the Orions deserved for this atrocity.

The Empire would serve the Orions their revenge, and they would serve it cold.

Hanging the phaser rifle around his neck with the shoulder strap, Kell raised his *mek'leth* and entered the killing box with Benitez beside him.

The field was thick with Orions and Klingons and Starfleet officers. Kell struck at an Orion who was firing his weapon, trying to hit one of the Klingons but succeeding in hitting only one of the other cowardly Orions. It was a glancing blow that spun the Orion around and into the blade of a waiting Klingon.

Remembering the lesson of his first sight of Gorath in action, Kell swung the blade upward, aiming for the unprotected throat. He willed the blade there and felt it cut through the fabric right under the helmet and right into the Orion underneath it.

So deep was the cut that Kell had trouble extracting his *mek'leth* from the dying Orion. He sensed rather than saw someone behind him. Turning his head as he pulled at the blade, Kell saw another Orion raising his rifle to him from less than two meters' distance.

In the hands of a master, the *mek'leth* was a weapon of great power and remarkable precision. In the hands of the merely competent, or even inept, it could still be deadly.

Benitez was actually better than competent with the blade, which he brought down hard on the Orion's left hand, which was steadying the barrel of the rifle. Catching the area between the glove and the forearm armor, the heavy blade tore straight through skin, sinew, and bone.

For a moment, the Orion looked dumbly at the stump before the blade of a Klingon caught him from behind.

Kell caught Benitez's eyes for just a moment before they were each caught back up in the battle again.

The Orions had no stomach for up-close fighting. They also tried too often to use their high-powered weapons at close range. As a result, they hit each other as often as they hit the defenders.

Kell's blade found an Orion. Then another.

As the enemy's ranks thinned, he spared a glance at the others. The landing party was doing well.

Kell knew that Starfleet self-defense training included instruction on a number of weapons, including blades and staffs. But some of the crew obviously had had additional experience, or great aptitude.

Kirk was faring well, as was Section Chief Brantley.

Kell noted that the others were all still alive.

Then he saw an Orion swinging his weapon like a club, striking Ensign Sobel on the back of the head. The human went down.

Then the Orion made his final mistake. Seeing the human incapacitated, the Orion tried to aim his weapon.

Parrish caught him in the elbow joint with her blade. He immediately dropped his rifle and she was able to swing the blade up and catch him in the underarm.

However, the blade became stuck between the chest and shoulder armor. And then Kell saw that the Orion was not incapacitated.

He was reaching for Parrish with his good hand.

Kell was immediately on the move, watching as the Orion grabbed her wrist and pulled her close. Before he could do whatever he had planned, Kell was there.

Instead of swinging his blade, he thrust it forward into the Orion's side, using the momentum of his charge to give the blow force. The blade slipped through the fabric, then between ribs, then traveled more than half of its length into the Orion's body.

Reflexively, the Orion released Parrish and fell to his knees. Kell knew the alien was dead, even if the lumbering coward did not yet know it himself.

He checked Parrish for damage and saw she was fine. She flashed him a look and then pulled her *mek'leth* free from the dying Orion's armor.

Then he and Parrish were fighting back-to-back, like Kahless and his great love Lady Lukura, who defeated five hundred warriors in the Great Hall of Qam-Chee.

As their blades found targets, Kell could see that the battle had turned. Yet the Orions continued to fight, like the one who had attacked Parrish—they were already dead but did not yet know it.

Kell saw some amazing displays of swordsmanship

by the Klingon warriors, and then the Orions were vanquished to the one. Looking across to the other line of defenders, he saw they had already finished their own enemies and were heading to help Kell's side.

By the time the first one reached them, however, the battle on the ground was done. The sound of a blast from above told Kell that the battle in the air was still raging.

He turned to see the two Klingon-piloted vehicles still darting around the lumbering Orion craft. Kell saw that Gorath still lived, as did the female pilot, which told him that the pilot whose craft he heard explode was the other male.

He also saw that three of the six gunners on the Orion craft were missing and its shield was flashing in and out of existence.

Another blast from Gorath's cannon and it disappeared altogether.

The two Klingon pilots turned around in tight arcs and rushed the Orion craft for what Kell was certain was the final time.

The end came quicker than even Kell expected as the Klingons fired a single blast each at the Orion craft, which did not explode so much as disintergrate underneath the pilot and surviving three gunners.

Kell watched them and the pieces of their cursed weapon fall and judged it a fitting end to their cowardly existences.

He took a quick inventory of the battlefield. All of the Orions were dead or dying and the losses to the defenders seemed remarkably light. He counted six dead Klingon warriors on their side.

And Ensign Sobel was still on the ground.

Captain Kirk and Parrish were standing over the officer and their faces told Kell that Sobel was dead.

He could see pain on the captain's face and rage on Parrish's.

Kell realized that Kirk had fought like a Klingon to protect a world full of people of Kell's blood, people who should have been Kirk's enemy.

At that moment, Kell knew that he could not kill Captain Kirk and would defend this human with his own life. He looked around at the Klingon warriors around him and saw his duty to the Empire—a duty greater than the cowardly murder of humans.

He saw a world of noble Klingons who were threatened by a real threat: greedy Orion monsters. He understood the dishonor of the Empire's lies about humans, about their nature and the danger they posed.

He had seen too much of their honor and their spirit. Suddenly, Kell was certain that the only way to extinguish that spirit would be to exterminate the humans. Just a few months ago, he would have thought such an atrocity would have been impossible in the Empire, which sought victory and glory but not wanton destruction.

Months ago he believed that the humans were weak, cowardly, and deceitful. Months ago he believed the Empire needed to strike first to prevent the human plague from overtaking the galaxy. Months ago he believed that the Empire was stronger than the Federation, but that the Klingon Infiltrators had to hide their faces to compensate for the humans' own underhanded tactics. Kell had believed that when he hid his true face he was merely doing what was necessary to protect the Empire.

He had believed many lies, but he now saw them for what they were. And he would not be a party to the Federation's destruction.

And for now, he had found a battle worthy of whatever was left of his honor.

Chapter Seventeen

"CAPTAIN," Acting Science Officer Parker said. Justman realized that that was the first time any of the crew had called him by that title. It sounded wrong to his ears. The ship had only one captain, Captain Rodriguez.

He nearly corrected the lieutenant, but checked himself when he saw Lieutenant Parker looking at him with respect and hope. The crew needed to believe they had a capable leader. He would not dispel that illusion and the hope it gave them. He knew the Klingons would take care of that soon enough.

"I have something on long-range scanners, headed this way," Lieutenant Parker said.

"Another Klingon ship?" Justman said.

There was an old Starfleet joke in which a ship's captain calls down to engineering and says, "Damage?"

The chief engineer replies, "No thanks, Captain, we have plenty."

Klingons, he thought to himself. *No thanks, we have plenty.*

He approached the science station. "Is it the Klingons, Ms. Parker?" he said as the lieutenant looked into the viewer.

"I don't know....I don't think so, sir. In fact, this is impossible," she said.

"What is?" Justman said, impatience creeping into his voice.

"Whatever it is, it's moving fast—warp six," she said.

"Warp six!" he replied. That *was* impossible.

"Is it on an intercept course?" he said.

"Yes, it will be here in twenty-four minutes. And sir, I have traced its point of origin. It took a minute because the speed—"

"Where is it coming from?" Justman interrupted.

"Earth, sir," she said.

Justman heard the sharp intake of breath from everyone in the control room, including himself.

He suddenly had an idea of what was intercepting them. It was impossible but he was not about to question good fortune, which seemed to be in extremely short supply today.

"Sir, we're being hailed. It's a Starfleet signal, but I don't recognize—"

"On screen," Justman called out.

The starfield and planet on the viewscreen were replaced by the face of a man in a Starfleet uniform, an admiral's uniform.

"This is Admiral William M. Jefferies in command of

the starship *U.S.S. Constitution,* designation NX-1701. The people back at Command thought you could use some help out here."

Justman could not keep the smile from his face and heard a cheer break out behind him.

"This is Lieutenant Commander Robert H. Justman, acting commander of the *U.S.S. Yorkshire.* It's an honor...sir."

Justman had never met Admiral Jefferies before, but he knew the man's reputation, though "legend" would be a better word.

Lately, Jefferies had become known as the father of the *starship* program to create the next generation of spacecraft. Like everyone else in the fleet, Justman had known that the *Constitution* was the prototype, but it was supposed to be almost a year from launch.

The *Constitution* was said to have high-speed warp engines, a crew capacity of over four hundred, and the ability to go *years* between stops. Some called the starships merely improved spaceships, but Justman knew that was like calling a photon torpedo an improved firecracker.

"We have received your log transmissions. You and your crew have done some amazing work out there. The honor is mine," Jefferies said.

Just a few minutes later, Justman saw what would remain the most beautiful sight of his life when he watched the *Constitution* appear on the viewscreen. Though the basic design—primary and secondary hulls with dual nacelles—was familiar, it had a graceful strength and a long-legged beauty that made Justman forget to breathe for a moment.

It was a ship of dreams, he remembered thinking, and it had come to save them.

Twenty-five years later, Admiral Robert H. Justman stared out his window. He decided he was doing altogether too much of that lately. From that window, he knew that others could see a dramatic and beautiful view of the San Francisco Bay and the Golden Gate Bridge.

When Justman looked out the window, however, he saw the past, a past that he now felt slipping away. He did not doubt that he might live to see the Federation's last days.

Even when things had been at their darkest at the battle of Donatu V, the worst prospect he and his ship had faced was the loss of their lives and control of the planet below them—terrible, to be sure, but not the end of everything.

...because the end of everything was impossible. The Federation was too strong, not just in military might, but in its principles. Cooperation made it strong. Respect for other peoples and other worlds made it strong.

Infinite diversity in its limitless combinations made it strong. Certainly, nothing could destroy that strength. It was truly impossible.

But a career that spanned more than three decades had taught Justman that nothing was impossible.

And in retrospect his belief that the Federation would stand forever seemed painfully naïve. The fact was that it was a newborn in political terms.

At less than a century old, it had endured only a fraction of the time that the Roman Empire had survived, much less than Great Britain, or even the United States of America.

Had he and others doomed the Federation because of

their foolish belief that it was invulnerable? Had that belief turned to arrogance that made them believe that because an idea was right, it was automatically powerful? That some truths were so obvious that they would somehow protect themselves?

The Starfleet readiness report told him that he might well fail in his duty to protect those ideas, those truths.

In the past, he had thought he had failed only to be later rescued by others, or by circumstance.

The *U.S.S. Constitution* had reached Donatu V before the three Klingon battle cruisers. Together, the *Yorkshire* and the incredible starship had held the Klingon until more Starfleet vessels could arrive.

And by then, more Klingon ships had arrived.

The battle was long and there were many sacrifices, too many. The *Constitution* was one of them. It went from being the prototype, a ship of dreams, to a badly damaged hulk and as a result would not be the first starship to be officially launched.

Yet they had survived, if not prevailed. At the time, Justman had thought the peace they had made was better than an outright victory. It had allowed the Klingons to keep their dignity and the Starfleet force to save many lives.

But somehow it had brought them to this, to the edge of destruction—the destruction of everything. All because he had not understood his enemy.

He understood the Klingons better now. As a result, he did not have to wonder what the Federation worlds would suffer during an extended war and what they would suffer in defeat. He knew.

And that knowledge pursued him in his nightmares,

like the face of a nameless Starfleet officer he had seen floating in space twenty-five years ago.

The battle was not over. In fact, it had yet to begin in earnest.

And there was a lesson he had learned from Captain Rodriguez, and Captain Shannon, and Admiral Jefferies, and countless officers in the service since. That lesson was that the struggle was not over until the last option found, the last ounce of reserve used, the last sacrifice made.

Justman had been surprised too many times in his career to rule out another surprise. He had seen too many opportunities created by better men than he to think that there were no solutions out there.

Until one of those solutions came, he would do his job and his duty to the best of his ability. And when they did come, he vowed to be ready.

"Admiral," his yeoman's voice sounded on the intercom.

"Yes," he said.

"They need you in the situation room," she said.

"I am on my way. Have Lieutenant West meet me there," Justman said.

A moment later, he left his office and the Golden Gate Bridge behind him.

Lieutenant West reached Admiral Justman in the corridor. The admiral nodded to him and motioned him to follow.

West had never been inside the Starfleet situation room before. This location was not on the cadet tour. In fact, he had never seen so much as an image of the room.

West was surprised by how small it seemed. The table had chairs for about a dozen people, with a large computer console on one side of the rectangular table. Just past the other end of the table, a large viewscreen dominated the far wall.

West recognized the people sitting around the table, not because he had met them before, but because there were few fleet admirals in the service and every first-year cadet knew who they were.

Yet when he was a cadet, he had sat in judgment of them, criticized their past decisions, called them warmongers and worse. The men at this table had fought some battles, yes, but they had also made many peaceful first contacts. They had made many discoveries, and sacrifices, and had fulfilled their and Starfleet's mission.

Part of that mission was to protect the Federation. They had certainly done that. And now, he knew, they were the best chance for the Federation's survival.

West realized now that he was able to criticize them not because they had fought, but because they had won. And by winning, they had created an atmosphere of safety and security within the Federation. In that atmosphere, people believed that not only were those two things the basic right of all beings—but those rights could never be seriously challenged.

Well, the Klingons were raised in a different atmosphere. And they were not only about to make that challenge, but they were in a position to win it.

The lieutenant had once believed that understanding would eventually eliminate war and the fear that caused it. Now, he understood the Klingons fairly well. He understood who they were, what drove them, and what they were capable of. He understood and he was terrified for the future.

There were no introductions. Admiral Justman and West simply sat, and then a young lieutenant commander sitting at the computer console started speaking.

"A Klingon battle cruiser has entered Federation space," the officer said. He hit a button on his console and a graphic of the border of Federation space appeared on the viewscreen.

The lieutenant commander stood up and walked to the viewer, pointing to a red dot on the Federation side of the border.

"They crossed here," he said.

There was something odd about that, but West could not put his finger on it.

Admiral Justman could, however, and spoke up immediately, "They crossed practically right on top of an automated sensor array?"

"Fortunately, yes," the young officer said.

"I'm not so sure," Justman said. "They can see our arrays from a sector away. This was no accident. They wanted us to see them."

"Is it the beginning of the invasion?" one of the junior admirals said.

"With one ship?" Justman asked. "There's something wrong here." He studied the map for a moment.

"System 7348," Admiral Justman said finally. "It's near 7348. Perhaps they are making a pickup at the Orion mine there."

Justman stood and looked at the head of the table, where Admiral Solow had sat. "Permission to send the *Enterprise* after them, sir."

It struck West odd that Justman answered to anyone. Intellectually he knew it had to be true, but seeing it still surprised him. Of course, if you were going to answer to anyone, it might as well be a legend.

Admiral Solow nodded his head. The word was given and the meeting was over.

On the way out, West found himself thinking about a number of things he had been meaning to do for some time. He decided that he had put one of them off for too long. It was time to take decisive action.

Chapter Eighteen

KIRK'S COMMUNICATOR BEEPED. He reached for it and flipped it open.

"Kirk here," he said.

"Captain, this is the *Enterprise*," Spock's voice said.

"Mr. Spock," Kirk said. "Your timing is impeccable."

"Are you in danger?" Spock asked.

"Not at the moment, Spock. What made you come?" Kirk said.

"We tracked the explosion of the shuttle with sensors and deduced that the Orions knew of your presence," Spock said. "I will tell the transporter to prepare—"

"No, Spock, we're not finished down here," Kirk said.

"We have just received orders from Admiral Justman to intercept a Klingon battle cruiser that has violated Federation space in this sector," Spock said.

A Klingon ship in Federation space could do a lot of

damage, Kirk thought. And the *Enterprise* was the only ship in the sector.

"Then the *Enterprise* will have to intercept," Kirk said.

"Then prepare for transport, Captain," Spock said.

"No, Spock. We still have a mission to complete here," Kirk said.

"Captain," Spock said in his perfectly reasonable tone. "Command thinks the Klingon ship may be coming to pick up dilithium from the mine. Logically speaking, if we stop the Klingons, there will be no danger of that pickup being made."

"Perfectly logical, but I have my doubts about that," Kirk said. "In any case, the mine still presents a danger to the planet and its indigenous population. Interesting people, by the way, Mr. Spock. I think that anthropology will have a field day down here."

"Captain, perhaps—" Spock began.

"We're not leaving, Mr. Spock, and you have your orders from Command," Kirk said.

"Very well. Can we beam down any additional personnel or resources?" Spock said.

Kirk thought about it. No, he would not put any more crewmen at risk.

"Not necessary. We have found some...local resources. But we have one crewman to beam up. Ensign Sobel did not make it," Kirk said.

"Understood," Spock said. "I will inform the transporter room."

"You are just going to leave Jim and the others down there?" McCoy said, his voice raised.

Spock called on his Vulcan control. "Doctor, I am

going to follow the captain's orders and the orders of Starfleet Command."

"But, Jim—" McCoy began.

"Doctor," Spock said, raising his own voice slightly. Unlike the doctor's, his was not an emotional move. It was a calculated one and had the desired effect. The doctor was immediately silent. He was also looking at Spock in surprise, no doubt surmising that he had just witnessed the Vulcan equivalent of an emotional display.

Spock noted with satisfaction that his logical action had worked.

"Sir," Uhura said. "The transporter room reports that Ensign Sobel is on board."

Spock nodded and said, "Mr. Sulu, please lay in a course for the Klingon vessel, maximum warp."

"Maximum warp, aye," Sulu said.

The helmsmen immediately broke orbit and prepared for warp. Clearly, he had laid in the course in advance. *Efficient,* Spock noted. And efficiency was important so the *Enterprise* could return as quickly as possible to System 7348.

"Lieutenant Uhura, open a hailing frequency to the Klingon ship," he said.

After a few seconds, she reported, "No response, sir."

"Keep trying," Spock said. The most efficient course he could conceive would be to convince the Klingon commander via subspace transmission to return to Klingon space. Then the *Enterprise* could immediately return to System 7348.

Unfortunately, Spock's study had shown him that the Klingons showed concern for efficiency only when it came to achieving their military objectives. And Spock doubted that returning to the Empire without incident would serve any of the Klingon vessel's objectives.

"We are being hailed by the Federation Starship *Enterprise*," the communications officer said.

Karel felt his blood burn in his veins. A vessel full of Starfleet cowards was waiting for them. It was within reach. The beginning of his vengeance was within reach.

The destruction of a single Earther ship would not satisfy his warrior's craving for his enemy's blood, but, he reckoned it would be an excellent start.

Turning his glance down toward Klak, he saw instantly that the Klingon's blood did not burn. He wondered if Klak's blood carried anything other than plots and his scheming plans for his own glory.

"Ignore their hails," Klak said. "Koloth, are they on an interception course?"

"Yes," Koloth said.

"Excellent," Klak said.

For a moment, Karel hoped that Klak would give the word and commit them to the only honorable course.

"Sensor operator," Klak said, "How many systems are within our reach before the Earthers arrive?"

Karel's hopes rose again. Perhaps the battle cruiser *D'k tahg* would strike some real blows for the Empire.

"Seven systems," came the reply.

"Describe them," Klak said.

As the sensor operator listed the astronomical characteristics of each system, Karel wondered what the commander was after.

"Stop," Klak said, and the sensor operator ceased his inane speech. "A red supergiant?"

"Yes, but the system is dead," the sensor operator replied.

"Perfect," Klak said. "Full speed to the red star."

Karel shook his head. Suddenly he felt sure that battle was not in Klak's plans for today. True, he had himself heard the orders from Command. They wanted the *Enterprise* detained.

But certainly destruction would detain them. And no one in command would question a commander who won such a victory.

Karel's blood was filled with desire to challenge Klak himself. Yet, he knew he would not. As the new captain's personal guard, he would not sacrifice honor to satisfy his own desires. He would do his duty and not raise a hand to Klak.

Catching movement in his peripheral vision, he saw Koloth scowling at the commander. Suddenly, Karel was certain that Koloth was thinking of his own challenge.

He had sensed Koloth's strength and purpose before. Karel knew that the challenge would come. And he thought it would come soon.

Karel and the rest of the landing party watched Ensign Sobel's body as the ship's transporter beam took it.

There was a long moment of silence after Sobel disappeared, then the captain explained that the *Enterprise* had been called away to investigate a Klingon incursion into Federation space.

For a moment, Kell wondered if the war was beginning, but then rejected the idea. It was too soon. And when it came, it would not be a single ship in Federation space, but an entire fleet.

"We still have a mission," Kirk said. "This planet—"

Then the ground began to shake. At first it was a slight tremor that seemed to pass. Kell noted that Parrish had her tricorder out and was studying it intensely.

She was still studying it when she was thrown violently to the ground by a sudden and intense shaking of the ground.

Kell's own feet felt the ground swell for a moment, then toss him down as well. His face pressed into the dirt, Kell felt the ground shake more violently than before, much more violently even than the shaking they had experienced when they first arrived.

Then the ground began not only to shake, but to move. Kell had seen oceans, though of course he had never swum in one. But he had seen the way the water moved and swelled.

That was what the ground was doing under him now, except it was much more violent than the relatively placid movement of the water he had seen.

The roar was deafening, its force pounding against his ears.

His body was tossed from side to side, thrown up and down. He tried to search out the rest of his squad but found that the shifting ground made it impossible to focus on anything for long.

He caught glimpses of trees falling nearby. He also saw the ground splitting and opening. Though he was keenly aware of these dangers, he also knew that he could do nothing to avoid them.

Even though he knew the noise and violence of the ground's movement was altering his perception of time, it seemed as if the shaking continued endlessly.

Then it began to subside. It was not a sudden, or even a quick process, but he gradually felt the ground settle as if after expending its awesome power it was tiring.

Kell saw that Kirk was on his feet first. He quickly inspected himself for damage and rose. He saw that Parrish was unharmed, as was Benitez, and Clark and Jawer.

"Everyone all right?" Kirk asked.

"Yes, sir," they replied.

"Of course, I think my hearing loss is going to be permanent," Benitez said to Kell.

Then Kell saw the Klingons gathering a few meters away. They were studying the ground. Kirk rushed over and Kell and the others followed.

Gorath and the others were on a rise, staring down at the ground beyond them. When Kell stepped up, he had to look for a moment to see what they were looking at. Then he saw. Klingon warriors, or parts of them, were sticking up through the dirt.

Obviously, a fissure had opened, swallowed some of the Klingons, and closed again.

Gorath did not hide his anger or his grief.

Finally, he looked up at Captain Kirk and said, "Your people and mine. We can stop this?"

Kell translated, and Kirk said, "Yes."

"What do we do?" the Klingon leader asked.

Chapter Nineteen

WITH A COMBINATION OF tricorder readings and reports from Gorath's scouts, the two leaders were able to piece together a clear picture of where the Orions stood. Gorath had been watching the Orions for some time and estimated they had nearly two hundred personnel on the planet.

Perhaps sixty of those now lay on the battlefield. That left one hundred and forty. Just over one hundred of those were already on the move, no doubt looking for the Klingons and the landing party. It seemed the Orions were determined to crush them quickly.

"My warriors do not *crush easily*," Gorath had said. "We will face and defeat them."

"My people can shut down the mine, but you cannot face a hundred armed Orions, even with your weapons," Kirk said.

Kell judged the captain was right. Gorath had only eight warriors left after the last battle and the earthquake. Even Klingons—great Klingons—might be overwhelmed by the Orions' greater numbers.

Gorath simply smiled. "We have many brothers, Captain." Then he made a loud whistle and suddenly nearly a hundred more Klingons appeared from the forest.

"They are from other villages. I sent for them before the battle began," Gorath said.

"Looks like the cavalry is here, Flash," Benitez said from beside him.

Kell did not respond. Instead, he looked in wonder at the Klingons as they approached. Their leader walked up to Gorath and the two began conferring.

The Klingons all wore *mek'leths* around their waists, and Kell felt like he was looking at one of the ancient armies of Qo'noS. He longed to join them, to throw off the burden of his dishonorable mission for the Empire.

For a moment he indulged in the fantasy of doing so, but knew he could not. He had a new duty to Captain Kirk, to whom he owed his life. And he could do more for these Klingons by smashing the Orion mining operation. If he survived that he would have plenty of time to figure out if it was even possible for him to live out his life with honor and dignity.

It was settled, Captain Kirk and Gorath shook hands again and separated, each returning to his own group. A single Klingon scout who knew the Orion installation would accompany the Starfleet officers.

Kell realized that separating the two forces made

sense on a number of levels. A battle could have but one leader and both men were clearly used to command.

Turning away from his Klingon brothers, Kell faced the captain, who looked at the assembled squad.

"You did very well today, but we have more to do. The Orion mine still poses a great threat to this planet and every person on it. It is up to us to persuade them to abandon this world," Kirk said.

"Persuade them, sir?" Chief Brantley said.

"In the strongest possible terms. In the event that they insist on following their dangerous course, we will have to take it upon ourselves to put a stop to the operation. This will not be easy. It will no doubt be a fortified structure with at least forty Orions guarding it," he said. He paused and gave them a grim smile. "On the other hand, after what I saw today, I would not bet on the Orions."

Then Kirk addressed Kell. "Mr. Anderson, I need you to stay close to me and our guest," he said. Kell took a place between the captain and the Klingon scout as they headed in the direction of the Orion mine.

It was only after they had taken a few steps that Kell realized he was still wearing the *mek'leth* he had used in the battle. A quick glance around told him that the captain was wearing his, as were Brantley and the others.

For a moment, he had a flash of insight into what the Federation and Empire might accomplish if they could somehow find a way to join forces.

He reached for the hilt and tested comfortable weight of the ancient and honored weapon. *Yes,* he

Kevin Ryan

thought. *I would not wager much on the Orions' chances today.*

"Mr. Spock, I have the Klingon commander," Lieutenant Uhura announced.

"Really," Spock said, raising an eyebrow. They had been hailing the Klingon vessel continuously for an hour and the Klingons had chosen not to respond.

Spock quickly calculated how long the *Enterprise* had until it intercepted the Klingon vessel. Eight minutes and forty-two seconds. Curious that the Klingon had waited until now to speak to them.

Logically, there was only one way to determine the Klingon's intentions.

"Open channel, Lieutenant," Spock said.

A moment later, a Klingon face filled the main viewscreen.

"This is Captain Klak of the Klingon Defense Force vessel *D'k tahg*," the Klingon said.

"This is Spock of the *U.S.S. Enterprise.* You are in violation of Federation space."

"You are a Vulcan," the Klingon said, with some surprise in his voice.

"Yes," Spock replied. "What is the nature of your business?"

"We have experienced a technical and navigational failure. We are here by...accident."

Spock heard the doctor mutter under his breath. The doctor's intimation was biologically impossible, since Klingons did not communicate with that portion of their anatomy. However, Spock agreed that it was likely the Klingon was lying.

208

Vulcan turned to the officer at the science station. "Sensors?"

"Nothing unusual on the Klingon vessel, sir," the junior science officer replied.

"Our scans show nothing unusual on your ship," Spock said to the Klingon.

"I said we have a malfunction," the Klingon said, raising his voice. Spock recognized the tone as threatening. Logically, if the Klingon was trying to threaten him, he did not necessarily intend hostile action. Of course, that did not mean the Klingon would not act with hostility if pressed.

"We will be there shortly. At that time, we can offer you assistance and escort you back to Klingon space," Spock said.

"We do not need your assistance," the Klingon said.

"You just indicated that you were still experiencing a malfunction. We can send an engineering team to assist in your repairs," Spock said. "Logically—"

The Klingon seemed furious, and shouted, "If a single one of you tries to board this ship, we will destroy you!"

Spock studied him impassively for a moment, which seemed to make the Klingon angrier. "I have only offered assistance. You, however, have violated standing agreements between the Federation and the Klingon Empire. Your presence is an act of war."

"Are you threatening me, Vulcan?" the Klingon said.

"I am merely pointing out—"

"I will not be threatened by you!" the Klingon shouted. A moment later, his face was replaced by the familiar starfield.

"You do seem to have a way with people, Mr. Spock," the doctor said from behind him.

The Vulcan ignored the comment.

"The Klingon vessel?" Spock asked the junior science officer, who took a moment to check the science station viewer.

"The ship is still heading for the red-giant system, sir," the officer replied.

The Klingon was lying, that much was clear. Thus, it was difficult to formulate a rational basis for his actions. If the Klingon's actions defied logic, perhaps an emotional analysis would be helpful.

Spock turned to the doctor, who was standing over his right shoulder. "Doctor, do you have any thoughts?"

McCoy seemed surprised to be asked. "I can't tell you what he's doing here or what he wants, but I can tell you that he seems inexperienced and lacks confidence. He seemed upset that you were questioning him, as if the insult were personal."

The Vulcan nodded. The doctor's analysis was logical, yet not immediately useful. For the moment, he had little choice but to track the Klingon ship and insure that it did not threaten any Federation interests. However, that seemed unlikely since it was headed for a remote and uninhabited system.

The most serious danger at the moment was to the captain. He was on a planet with an entrenched and no doubt heavily armed enemy. And given Kirk's impetuous nature, Spock doubted he was taking reasonable precautions for his own safety.

For the moment, there was nothing Spock or the *Enterprise* could do but wait.

Karel's blood still burned. Klak's communication with the Vulcan had been an embarrassment. He had accomplished nothing and had let the Vulcan antagonize him.

Honor demanded that he not raise a hand to Klak, and he would do as honor required, but he thought that, in this case, honor was a very difficult master.

Chapter Twenty

THE INFORMATION Lieutenant West wanted appeared on the screen. He said a silent thanks to Admiral Justman, whose order had given West top-level security clearance and access to virtually any file or piece of information in the Starfleet computer system.

He committed the information to memory and got up from his desk. The watch officer gave him a strange look. It was the first time he had left his office this early since he had accepted the post to the admiral's staff.

In the corridor, West noted that the halls seemed more crowded than usual. Then he realized that he usually left his office when most of the people currently in the corridor were asleep.

He also realized how little of the Starfleet complex he

had explored. Since his own quarters were close to his office, he had had little reason to do so. As he discovered, the residence areas were huge. Nevertheless, he was finally able to find the hallway he was looking for. Then it was a simple matter of reading door signs until he found the right number.

When he reached the right door, he realized that he could not hesitate for a moment. Otherwise, he might not be able to do what he had come to do.

The stars favor the bold, he thought, and pressed the button outside the door.

A moment later, the doors opened and Yeoman Hatcher leaned out. She had an odd look on her face, as if she were…what? Annoyed?

"Hello, Yeoman Hatcher," he said. "I'm Lieutenant West."

He saw no recognition in her eyes.

"From Admiral Justman's staff," he added.

There it was, recognition, and something else. *Was* she annoyed? The expression almost looked like suspicion.

"What do you want?" she asked.

West swallowed. He had been busy on his thesis his last year at the Academy and had let the social side of his life slide. But he had done this before and he didn't remember it being this difficult.

And Yeoman Hatcher had smiled at him on a number of occasions before her leave. He was sure of it.

He felt like he had left a circuit open on his atomic pile and was losing power. He had to do something to get the conversation on track.

"How was your vacation?" he asked.

"My what?" she asked.

"Your vacation.... You were on leave," he said.

She studied him for a moment. "It was...restful," she said in a cold voice.

Was she upset that he had checked up on her? Or had he just caught her on a bad day?

He was committed now. He decided to see this through to the end. "Have you had dinner yet?" he asked, knowing that she had not.

"No," she said flatly. The tone did not invite anything more, but West was determined.

"Have you ever heard of the Six Oh Two club?" he asked.

"No, what is it?" she said impatiently.

"It is a bar, in town...would you like to go there?... Tonight?...With me?" he said.

For the first time an emotion he understood crossed her face. She was surprised.

"You want me to accompany you to dinner?" she asked.

"Yes, I mean, if you wouldn't—" he began.

"No," she said, in her flat tone.

It didn't make sense, he thought. She *had* smiled at him.

"Maybe another time then," he said, trying to retain some dignity in his voice.

"No," she said. "I do not wish to."

Then she pushed past him and said, "I have to go."

Dumbfounded, he watched her stride down the corridor.

Well, he thought, *that is one regret I can cross off my list.*

She must have been having a bad day. Yet, she didn't

seem to want to hear from him again. He had been turned down before, but the girls had usually been at least polite.

As he watched her disappear down the corridor, he realized what else was bothering him. It was her walk. It seemed different somehow.

Maybe she pulled something, or injured herself on leave, he thought as he headed back to his office.

For the first time, Kell saw the Orion installation, rising above the trees. It did not look like much. A simple prefabricated structure of five or six levels, barely large enough to house the two hundred Orions who lived there.

"Most of the structure will be underground, sir," Leslie Parrish said from behind him, studying her tricorder.

Of course, Kell thought. *She grew up on a mining planet.*

Kirk stopped and turned to listen to her.

"That is just the residence area. Nine-tenths of the operation—the actual mine, the warp reactors—and the heavy equipment are all underground," she said.

Their scout pointed to the residence and said, "A tunnel leads from that building to the upper level of the mining facility."

Kell translated and Kirk nodded. "Perhaps we can catch some of them napping," he said. "Let's go."

A few minutes later, the landing party was peering over a small rise at the front of the residence, which was perhaps two hundred meters away. Kell could see a large, fully-enclosed tunnel that led to another, single-level structure.

Kirk studied the scene.

"Defenses?" Kirk asked.

Kell repeated the question to the scout, who replied, "They have the same weapons as the green skins use, but they are larger and fire by themselves."

"Automated cannons, Captain," the Klingon said to Kirk.

"Our friend wouldn't happen to know their positions?" Kirk asked.

Before Kell could reply, he noticed that the Klingon scout was moving: he sneaked over the rise and darted toward the building.

"What is he doing?" Kell heard Benitez exclaim from nearby.

Then Kell watched as one of the automated cannons popped out of a panel in the building near the ground.

The cannon fired directly at the place where the Klingon was a moment before. It made a large crater in the ground, and Kell understood that it was much more powerful than even the platform-based cannons the Orions had used.

Then Kell realized what the Klingon was doing. He was showing them the location of the defenses.

Before the thought had finished forming in Kell's head, Kirk was already in motion, raising his phaser rifle and firing it at the cannon.

It exploded with remarkable force, shattering several square meters of the façade of the building.

By then the Klingon scout was racing back and forth across the open field in front of the building. More cannons appeared and tried to track him.

Kell was already on his feet, as were Brantley and the rest of the squad. They followed Kirk into the open. Suddenly there were a dozen cannons firing at the various moving targets.

Kell saw Kirk roll and come up firing at another cannon, which exploded. He realized that the cannons must be unshielded. It made sense. The Orions thought their only enemies were primitives.

Typical Orion arrogance, Kell thought as his own phaser rifle found its mark. Then Kell was moving again.

He saw cannon after cannon disintegrate under the teams' combined fire. Kell found one more target himself before they were all gone.

He felt a hand patting him on the shoulder. It was Benitez, who smiled and said, "Flash, this is almost unfair. Maybe we should tell the others to take a break. You and I can take care of the rest."

Kell studied his roommate for a moment and then replied seriously, "You think it will require both of us?"

The human laughed out loud and said, "You're okay, Flash. You're really coming along."

By then the scout had rejoined the group.

"Thank you," Kirk said to the Klingon, who needed no translation and nodded.

Kirk turned to the group and said, "Let's get inside and try the direct approach."

Kell approved. A direct assault was best. The Orions were not warriors in any real sense. They only fought when they had great advantage. A direct show of strength might well make their resistance crumble.

The team crossed the field to the tunnel. Inside, they could see a few Orions scurrying through the transparent aluminum structure. The Orions saw them and hurried on. As the Klingon suspected, they had no heart for a fight.

Ensign Jawer was the first at the tunnel's exterior access door. The door was large enough for Orions and looked very solid.

"It's locked," Jawer said. Already the ensign was trying to pry open the control panel.

"Give me a minute," he said. "I might be able to—"

Kirk put a restraining hand on Jawer and said, "Stand back, everyone."

Everyone fell back a few meters and Kirk leveled his phaser rifle at the door. He fired and the door blew inside the tunnel, twisting into a ball of metal.

Kirk stepped through the door opening. Chief Brantley did the same, motioning the squad to follow. Before he stepped through himself, Brantley turned back and said, "And that, recruits, is why *he* is the captain."

Stepping inside, Kell was careful not to touch any of the still red-hot metal around the door. In the tunnel he saw Kirk and Brantley already running at full speed toward the mining complex.

Kell was immediately following them at a run himself. It was only after a few steps that he saw why they were running. At the end of the tunnel, perhaps a quarter of a kilometer away, a blast door was closing. It was large, the full hundred-meter width of the tunnel and half that high. It was moving slowly but was already more than halfway closed.

Even as he gave the run everything he had, he could see that they would not make it. The door shut with a deep and resounding clang when they were still fifty meters away from it.

Kirk came to a stop, using a unique array of human expletives.

Jawer sized up the door and said, "Give me a minute with it. I might be able to get it open."

The words were barely out of Jawer's mouth when Kell heard a familiar hiss. He was trying to place it when he heard the captain yell, "Overload timer, drop!"

Then Kell was diving for the floor and covering his head and neck with his arms.

The explosion was loud in the enclosed tunnel, and he felt the hot blast pass over his head.

After a few seconds, he judged it safe to get up. As he did, he surveyed the door. He could see where the three explosive bolts on each side of the door had detonated. The result was that the heavy door had fused solidly to the frame.

Kell counted the seven phaser rifles and did some quick calculations in his head. They might be able to blast through...if they had some extra power packs and a few months to spare.

No one said anything until the captain turned around and said, "Let's go back to the residence and see if we can find some answers there."

They moved quickly through the tunnel and saw the opening to the residence area. It was open, and there was no blast door.

They stepped inside, seeing a small amount of debris.

The tunnel had obviously focused the explosion into the residence and there were pieces of furniture and equipment nearby.

As the landing party and their Klingon scout stepped inside, Kell guessed they were in some sort of large recreation room. Despite the damage caused by the blast, he could still make out some of the equipment in the room.

He shuddered at the thought of what the Orions did for their entertainment.

"Look for a computer terminal," Kirk said, and the teams spread out, Kell and Benitez staying together. They found one terminal broken, then another.

Finally, he heard Jawer's voice call out: "I have one here, sir."

The rest of the landing party converged on Jawer's position. The ensign was huddled over the terminal. On the screen, there were some graphics that meant nothing to Kell and some Orion characters that he recognized but could not read.

"Anyone read Orion?" Kirk asked.

No one did.

"This terminal is pretty standard," Jawer said. "There should be a translation circuit."

Then the ensign hit a switch and the display changed to English words and numerals. Suddenly, Kell had a very bad feeling.

"It's a countdown," Kirk said. "For what?"

Then Kell recognized what he was looking at. It was a warp-core schematic.

"Two countdowns. They have some sort of pickup planned," Jawer said. Then he studied the screen again for a moment and said in a remarkably calm voice, "They have also set the warp reactor to go critical in just under an hour. Their pickup will come just before that."

"Can we stop it?" Kirk asked.

Jawer studied the schematic. "Yes, if we can get inside. The computer has taken all of the safety protocols offline. We would just need to reset the system manually, but I would have to be with the reactor. The computer's controls are locked out."

Kirk nodded. "If we can't get there, can we evacuate Gorath's people? How far away do we need to get?"

Jawer quickly manipulated the computer's controls, obviously trying to do the calculations.

Parrish stepped forward and said, "Sir, I grew up on a mining colony. The matter-antimatter explosion would likely not reach the surface. The problem is that when the core goes critical, it ejects down, straight into the central mine shaft. And because this is deep-core mining, that means it goes straight through the crust of the planet into the mantle, which is a combination of magma and silicate minerals. When the warp core explodes, it will cause tremendous pressure...there will be no safe place. The pressure will tear the planet apart in minutes."

Kirk took just a second to absorb this and said, "Then we need to stop the core from going critical."

Kell looked into the captain's eyes and saw that there was no question in Kirk's mind that they would accomplish this. Success was inevitable and getting there a matter of details. He wondered for a moment if this human had any Klingon blood in him.

Kirk turned to Kell and said, "Ask our guide if there is another way into the mine?"

Kell did and translated the scout's answer. "He says there is, sir, but he doesn't think you will like it."

Chapter Twenty-one

"THE KLINGONS are dropping out of warp and entering the system," Junior Science Officer Stern said. "The star is a red supergiant and the system is unexplored, sir. However, I am reading no life signs of any kind."

"He's taking us on a wild goose chase, Spock," McCoy said.

The Vulcan understood the meaning of the metaphor, if not its origin. "I quite agree," he said. "Unfortunately, there is little we can do but follow. We cannot allow a Klingon battleship free reign within Federation space and our orders prevent us from firing directly on the Klingon vessel unless we are fired upon."

"Meanwhile, Jim is on his own down there," McCoy said.

"Once again, Doctor, you demonstrate a very firm grip on the obvious," Spock replied.

"Approaching the system. We will reach its limits in four minutes, seventeen seconds," Lieutenant Stern said.

"Location of the Klingon vessel?" Spock asked.

"They are entering orbit around the star," the acting science officer said.

"If they get too close, perhaps that star will take care of our problem for us," McCoy said.

"Unlikely, Doctor. The red supergiant is among the coolest of the stars," Spock said. "The Klingons will likely be in no danger from it for the next one hundred million years."

Spock calculated the time until the very edge of the system.

"Mr. Sulu, drop out of warp on my mark," Spock said.

The Vulcan waited until he calculated that the *Enterprise* had reached the system's boundary. He waited a few more seconds, until they were inside the system limits. It added risk, because the ship could overshoot and collide with the star. Yet time was important now and he had great faith in Lieutenant Sulu's abilities.

"Mark," Spock said.

Sulu executed the maneuver immediately and flawlessly.

"We are point three five astronomical units from the star," Acting Science Officer Stern said.

"Excellent. Mr. Sulu, interception course with Klingon vessel. Full impulse," Spock said.

"Full impulse, aye," Sulu said.

After a few minutes, Lieutenant Stern said, "Interception in two minutes."

"Lieutenant Uhura, hail the vessel," Spock said.

"No response," Uhura said a few seconds later.

"Mr. Sulu, put us on a parallel course, two kilometers from the Klingon vessel," Spock said.

After less than a minute, Sulu reported, "We have established parallel course."

The viewscreen now showed the red star on the left-hand side and, above it, the Klingon ship.

"Still no response from the Klingons," Uhura said.

Spock saw that this situation could continue indefinitely. Logically speaking, only decisive action could speed its outcome.

The Vulcan stood. He had noted in the past that when Captain Kirk stood up in moments of stress, it seemed to increase the crew's confidence.

That confidence would be an asset now.

"Mr. Sulu, shield status?" he asked.

"Shields at maximum," Sulu replied.

"Arm a photon torpedo," Spock said.

He heard the doctor's sharp intake of breath.

"What about your orders, Spock?" the doctor said.

"I intend to follow them to the letter," Spock said. "Sulu, target the space three kilometers in front of the Klingon ship and fire at will."

There was a momentary hesitation as Sulu made the calculations and said, "Firing now."

Spock could see the torpedo's arc taking it in front of the Klingon ship and then the flash of the explosion.

"Status of Klingon ship?" Spock asked.

Lieutenant Stern studied the science-station viewer for a moment and then said, "They seem to be undamaged."

Spock turned to the doctor. "My orders were not to fire directly on the Klingon ship unless provoked. Consider that torpedo a communication of our seriousness."

"But the Klingons will see that as a challenge, Spock," McCoy said.

"Yes," Spock said. Now they would see how the Klingons responded. "Given what we know of Klingons, the commander will logically either answer the challenge or withdraw. Either way, we will see a timely conclusion to this situation."

All eyes were on the viewscreen. The Klingon ship stayed its course.

"The Klingons have their weapons powered, but they have not targeted us," Lieutenant Stern announced.

Good, Spock thought. Perhaps the Klingon vessel was not prepared to fight. Spock quickly calculated how long it would take to escort the vessel back to Klingon space at high warp and return to System 7348 to assist the captain.

"The Klingon is executing a maneuver," Stern said.

Spock watched as the Klingon vessel shifted its orbit. Oddly, however, it did not break away from the red supergiant it was orbiting. Instead, it was in a rapid descent toward the surface of the star.

"What's he doing, Spock?" McCoy said. "Whatever it is, it doesn't look logical."

Then Spock saw the logic of the maneuver.

"Pursue and match speed," he said as he strode over to the science station. Stern stepped aside and the Vulcan quickly recalibrated the shields for heat and a few narrow bands of radiation.

"Klingon vessel entering the outer layer of the star," Sulu said.

"Continue pursuit," the Vulcan said, his voice calm.

Nevertheless, he could see the bridge crew was concerned. After a slight hesitation, Mr. Sulu said, "Laying in an interception course now."

As the landing party stepped around the low-slung Orion building, Kell looked out and for a moment thought he was looking down into a great pit in Gre'thor, where the Klingon dishonored dead went.

This pit was enormous, no less than five kilometers across. It was also deep—how deep Kell could not yet tell from this distance.

Kirk led the landing party to some sort of loading platform that sat on the edge of the near side of the vast pit. When they reached the edge, Kell was able to look down and see into the depths; he was even more convinced that he was looking at a pit in Gre'thor.

The sides of the roughly circular pit showed rock that had been cut away. Because it was so wide and the planet's sun was nearly overhead, Kell could see very far down. Yet, he could not see the bottom, which disappeared into darkness.

The scout spoke to Kell and he said, "Captain, he says the entrance is down there."

Parrish stepped forward with her tricorder. "About five kilometers down, sir," she said. "That is where the large equipment and the warp reactor are."

She studied the tricorder for another moment. "It does not seem to be guarded, however. I'm not getting a concentration of life signs near the entrance."

Kirk nodded and was already moving, studying a large open-top platform. Kell immediately recognized the design as Orion. It looked like their weapons platforms except it was much larger—a rectangle of perhaps fifty meters in length—and it had no visible weapons. Just a pilot's console and a large, flat open space behind it.

"It is not armed, Captain," Parrish said, as if she were reading Kell's thoughts. "It's for hauling ore and minerals up from the mine. It will get us down to the Orions."

"Then let's go," Kirk said, stepping aboard. He was already studying the controls.

Parrish and the others quickly followed. "I can pilot it, Captain," she said.

With a nod from Kirk, Parrish took the controls. She turned back to the rest of the team and said, "Hold on to the railing—tight—and put your feet in the restraints. The ride can feel a bit rough if you aren't used to it."

Their Klingon scout told them he had to go. Kell understood. His people were fighting for their lives and he wanted to stand with them.

"Tell him thank you," Kirk said.

The Klingon nodded and quickly disappeared. The rest of the landing party quickly boarded the vehicle.

As Parrish piloted the large craft off the ground, Kell grabbed the railing with one hand and slipped the front of his boots into two metal cylinders bolted to the floor.

For such a heavy piece of equipment, Kell noted, the ride was smooth. It floated up a few meters and then slid over the edge of the pit.

Looking over the side, Kell felt a touch of vertigo. It seemed they were hanging over a bottomless abyss, which—he realized—for all intents and purposes, they were.

When the platform was in position, fully over the pit, Parrish turned back to smile at him and hit one of the controls.

And then the world dropped out from under him.

The platform immediately went into free fall. At first he thought something had gone wrong, but he saw Parrish calmly monitoring the readouts in front of her.

The fall seemed endless, and then they started to slow. Unlike the sudden fall, the deceleration was smooth, and then they were lined up with another platform.

Above and around the platform, Kell could see a huge opening—hundreds of meters across. There was also a huge amount of heavy equipment on the platform, ore haulers and others vehicles that he did not recognize.

Like the rest of the squad, Kell had his phaser rifle out and was scanning for Orions or automated defenses. He saw neither. Apparently, the Orions were elsewhere, and there were no other defenses, because it was inconceivable to them that the primitive people would ever reach this point.

For a moment, that struck his Klingon pride. Primitive or not, the people on this planet were Klingons, and the Orions knew that. Nothing should have been inconceivable.

Whatever happened, he would make sure the Empire learned of the Orion treachery. What sort of honorless monsters would tear an inhabited planet to pieces for the stones under its soil?

Battles were not fought and wars not powered by stones, even ones with the special properties of dilithium crystals. Wars were won with the strength of a warrior's blood, the courage in his heart, and the depth of his honor.

Parrish placed the vehicle down on the ground, and Kell found that he was relieved.

"Excellent work, Ensign," Kirk said to Parrish. "Very...fast."

"Thank you, sir," she said.

Kirk stepped off first and the others followed. Kell found himself next to Parrish.

"I thought you said growing up on a mining world was boring," he said to her.

She turned to him and said, "Even that trip gets old when you've done it enough."

Then she smiled and he returned it. Something passed between them, and Kell found himself thinking that a future might be somehow possible for him. As the thought took shape in his mind, he realized that it was extremely unlikely but not impossible. And he realized that in the image of himself in that nearly impossible future, he did not stand alone.

And then the moment had passed and the landing party was headed for the large opening to the Orion mining installation.

Spock watched as the Klingon battle cruiser skimmed the surface of the red star. Then the ship dipped lower and was swallowed up inside.

"That's impossible," McCoy said.

"Status of Klingon ship, Mr. Stern?" Spock said.

"I'm getting some readings," the junior science officer said. "But I can't be sure if it's them...there's a lot of interference."

"They must have been destroyed," McCoy said.

"Unlikely, Doctor. I suspect we are looking at a Klingon tactic with some history. Red supergiants are the least dense and among the coolest of all stellar formations, particularly in the surface areas. Theoretically, it is possible for a ship with adequate shielding to navigate within."

"Then they might slip around and escape from the other side. We'd never know," McCoy said.

"Precisely, Doctor," Spock said. "Mr. Sulu, pursuit course. Take us into the star, thruster speed only."

"Aye, sir," Sulu said as he executed the maneuver.

"Spock, you can't," McCoy said. "You said it was only *theoretically* possible for a starship to navigate inside one of those. Even if the Klingons have done this before, we haven't."

"You are quite right, Doctor. This will be a fascinating experiment," Spock said.

"Spock—" McCoy began, but then became absorbed by the surface of the red star that was rapidly filling the viewscreen.

The screen showed nothing but the star. A few seconds later, Spock felt a small tremor through the deck.

"We are inside the star," Lieutenant Stern said. "Temperature and radiation within shield limits."

Spock glanced at the doctor and saw that the human's

mouth was open as he stared at the screen in frank astonishment.

"Any sign of the Klingon ship?" Spock said.

"There's some interference, but...yes, I have him on scanners," Stern said.

"Continue pursuit course, Mr. Sulu," Spock said.

Chapter Twenty-two

KAREL SAW THE ORIONS on the catwalk above them first and fired his phaser rifle. He hit one, and then a second beam hit the other.

He turned to see that it was Parrish who had fired the second beam.

"Is that all the resistance?" Benitez said. "They know we're here."

"But they also know that the warp core is going to detonate in forty minutes," Kirk said. "I suspect they are preparing for their pickup."

The captain gestured to a nearby computer terminal. "Mr. Jawer, see if you can find out the quickest route to the warp core, and where the Orions are hiding."

Ensign Jawer was at the controls of the computer, his hands moving quickly and confidently over the console.

"I've got it, sir. The warp core is six hundred meters

in that direction," he said, pointing toward the main corridor leading away from the pit and deeper into the planet.

"What about the Orions?" Kirk said.

Jawer studied the readout for a moment. "They are in a protected transporter chamber. It's completely sealed off. They must have transported in. I think they are waiting for their pickup inside."

"Can you turn off the internal transporters? Seal them in?" Kirk asked.

"Done, sir," Jawer said.

"Let's move then, we don't have much time," Kirk said.

"Wait, Captain," Jawer said, running his hands over the controls again. "There is another designated beam-out site. There might be more there. I think this one is where they are storing the crystals."

"I'll go, sir," Kell found himself saying. Whatever happened, he would see that the Orions and their honorless masters never got their hands on the dilithium they wanted to trade an entire world of Klingons to possess.

"I'll go too," Benitez offered. Kell was pleased.

He was glad that he had resisted his initial urges to kill the human, who had turned out to be a good companion and brave.

Kell found he could even forgive Benitez's tendency to speak too much.

Kirk nodded, and Jawer quickly showed them the route to the second pickup site. It was fairly straightforward, and since it was near the edge of the pit they would not likely get lost.

"Let's move, we don't have a lot of time," Kirk said, leading the way.

Before they turned to go, Kell and Parrish caught each other's eyes. Parrish held her gaze on his and Kell saw something take shape in her eyes: it was his future.

"I don't think she's finished with you," Benitez said.

Kell didn't respond, though he knew it was true. He also knew that he was not finished with her.

Then he and Benitez were headed out at a run, keeping the abyss to their left for reference.

"Now we will slip away while the Federation ship spends the next month searching and waiting for us to emerge," Klak said, his voice full of self-satisfaction.

Karel still felt his blood burning. The red-giant maneuver had been used before to great effect, allowing a Klingon ship to hide and surprise an enemy.

This, however, was no doubt the first time in Klingon history that the maneuver had been used to cover an escape... worse, a retreat.

It was intolerable.

"The *Enterprise* is pursuing. They are inside the stellar mass," the sensor officer announced.

"What?" Klak said. "They cannot. No cowardly Earther commander would..."

"The commander is not an Earther," Koloth said, speaking Karel's own thoughts for him.

Klak brought his fist down on the command chair.

"Full thruster speed," Klak called out.

"At full speed now," the helmsman said.

"Prepare to engage impulse engines," Klak said.

Karel was shocked. Even given the relatively low density of the outer skin of the star, impulse speeds would be very dangerous.

Yet Klak was prepared to risk the ship...simply to run away *faster*.

"But—" the helmsman began.

"Do it!" Klak ordered.

Koloth's voice rang out, "Torpedo away," he said.

"What?" Klak said.

"I have fired a torpedo at the Federation ship, as you ordered," Koloth said.

"I did not order that!" Klak countered.

Koloth was calm. "Nevertheless, I have fired."

Klak looked ready to burst, as if he wanted to kill Koloth right now for the insubordination. Yet, even Klak knew that he did not have time. When the torpedo exploded, the chain reaction would be much more destructive than the torpedo itself. Already, he had lost precious seconds scowling at his weapons officer.

"Helm, full thruster speed for the surface of the star! Get us into space!"

Karel felt the movement of the ship with his feet. He saw the red haze of the interior of the star dominating the viewer. Then it began to lighten.

"Torpedo detonating," Koloth said.

An instant later, Karel felt the ship rock violently, then saw the familiar stars of open space.

"Damage report," Klak called out.

"Damage to sensors and secondary systems. Primary systems intact," came the report.

They had survived unharmed, Karel noted, because they had been very near the surface of the star and had been spared the full force of the stellar flare.

The Earthers, however, were still inside.

* * *

"Klingon vessel is arming a torpedo," Lieutenant Stern said.

Already on his feet, Spock turned and vaulted over the bridge railing, landing next to the science station— peripherally aware that he was pushing the doctor aside as he did it.

"Full thruster speed to the surface," Spock shouted as he grabbed the science-station controls from Lieutenant Stern.

For them to have even a chance to survive, Sulu would have to comply without question and forgo a helmsmen's instinct to execute evasive maneuvers when under torpedo fire.

Sulu's "Aye" told Spock that he was complying. That meant there was still a chance.

As quickly as he could, Spock focused all possible shield strength to the rear of the ship.

When the chain reaction began, they would need to be as far ahead of the solar flare as possible and make certain the shields did not immediately fail under the assault of energy.

Counting the elapsed time in his mind, Spock realized that they would not make the surface in time. Now the ship's survival depended entirely on the shields. They would either perform or fail.

Spock knew that given time, he could calculate their chances. Yet he knew that the matter would be settled before the calculations were complete.

Looking into the science-station viewer, Spock saw that the torpedo had detonated. The radiation reached the ship immediately and was easily repelled by the shielding.

Then the chain reaction began. Spock caught sight of the solar flare's leading edge just as it reached the *Enterprise*'s position.

Then the deck shook violently under his feet, and the bridge went completely dark as power failed.

Chapter Twenty-three

"ANY SIGN OF THE EARTHERS?" Klak shouted.

"No sign, but they did not make it out of the star," Koloth said.

"Then they are finished. Helm, take us back to Klingon space. Maximum speed. I am eager to leave the stink of this Federation behind us."

Eager to run from battle, Karel thought.

Klak stood and turned to the weapons console, where Koloth sat staring back at him.

"You challenge my leadership with your insubordination, Koloth, you challenge me," Klak said. His voice sounded strong, but Karel noted that the commander had made certain that Karel and the other guard, Ranc, were between him and the weapons officer.

"No, I challenge a weak and cowardly *Earther,* without the courage or honor to lead," Koloth said.

239

Klak glanced once to Ranc, who drew his *d'k tahg,* and then to Karel, who drew his own. Karel noted that Koloth had his own blade drawn and was staring at Klak and his two guards without fear.

It was a nearly hopeless battle, yet Koloth was obviously prepared to wage it.

Karel did not think about what he did next, he simply acted. Stepping in front of Klak, he reached out with his left hand and brought the back of it across Ranc's face.

The Klingon looked at him in surprise for a moment; then he understood the deadly insult. He lunged forward with the knife. The blow was clumsy but powerful, and Karel was barely able to deflect it.

Ranc, however, did not even see his counterstrike, a quick, powerful jab with his *d'k tahg.* The honored blade that was once his father's penetrated Ranc's uniform, and slid between his ribs and straight into the Klingon's chest.

Ranc clutched at the wound and then fell.

Karel pulled his blade out as the Klingon fell and turned to face Klak, who was looking at him incredulously.

"You are sworn to protect me!" the Klingon demanded.

"From any unequal challenge," Karel spat back. "I see nothing but a single honorable Klingon making a just challenge. It is more than you gave to Captain Kran when you murdered him."

"You cannot do this!" Klak shouted.

Another voice sounded. It was Koloth's, and said, "Do not worry about him, Klak. You should worry about me."

Koloth lifted his blade high.

Klak turned and shouted, "Withdraw your challenge or die!" Karel did not have to strain to hear the fear in Klak's voice.

Koloth smiled and said, "I will withdraw nothing but my blade from your lifeless body."

Klak lifted his own blade and lunged at Koloth. The weapons officer did not bother to sidestep. He met the charge head-on and, as he promised, plunged his *d'k tahg* into Klak's chest.

Karel thought it was over. Then he saw that Klak's blade had found its mark as well. It had pierced Koloth in the shoulder.

As Klak clutched him, dying, Koloth calmly pulled Klak's blade from the wound. Then he withdrew his own blade from Klak's chest and—as the Klingon sank to the deck—wiped it on Klak's uniform.

Then Koloth kicked Klak's body, rolling it over once, making room in front of the command chair.

Karel took a guard's position behind Koloth and said, "Congratulations, *Captain* Koloth."

Koloth turned to him and nodded. "Take your post, Bridge Weapons Officer Karel," he said.

Karel wanted to protest. He was not ready for that honor, yet he would not question Koloth's judgment on the bridge.

He simply nodded and took a position in front of the console.

He spared a look back at Koloth, who remained standing, showing no sign that he would seek medical attention for his wound.

Karel had no doubt that Koloth would finish the duty cycle just where he was, on his feet in front of his command chair.

Suddenly, he realized that he had a commander he would be honored to follow.

Let the Earthers tremble, Karel thought.

His time of vengeance was drawing near. He could feel it.

"It's up ahead," Benitez said, pointing to movement in the distance.

Equipment and various containers blocked the view, but Kell could make out the movement and occasional patches of green skin.

Kell knew they had better hurry. According to the computer countdown, the pickup was scheduled a full fifteen minutes before the warp-core failure.

The Klingon estimated that they had less than ten minutes left now. He wished he had a chronometer and cursed whoever decided that Starfleet officers didn't need them.

As they moved closer, Kell caught a better glimpse of the Orions. They were standing next to an ore hauler larger than but similar to the one that Parrish had used to lower them to the level of the mines. These Orions, he noted, were not combat troops and were not wearing armored suits.

The ore container they were unloading was full of large, rough crystals, which the Orions were moving with small, hand-controlled antigrav sleds to the large transporter platform, which sat thirty meters across from the hauler. Behind that was a control station of some kind, which no doubt provided controls for the transporter and the other heavy equipment in the area.

Kell and Benitez took a crouching position behind heavy cargo containers.

"I count six, Flash," Benitez said. "How about you?"

"Six, but there may be more to the right," Kell said,

pointing to the transporter and control area to the right. The area was partially obscured by the huge support beams that ran from the floor to the hundred-meter-tall ceiling.

"They look like no problem," Benitez said.

Kell nodded. "But let's not take any chances. We cannot let the Orions escape with their precious dilithium."

His roommate nodded, and they both took aim.

"Target the vehicle's antigrav pads," Kell said.

Benitez nodded, and both officers trained their phasers on one of the two circular pads at the bottom of the transport.

"On three," Benitez said.

"One," the Klingon said.

"Two," Benitez replied.

Then together, they said, "Three."

The phaser rifles in their arms let loose their deadly red energy simultaneously. The heavy vehicle rocked when the beams struck but, surprisingly, absorbed the energy.

They kept their fire trained on the antigrav pads and watched the metal around it change shape and begin to buckle.

A few seconds later the pads flashed and something exploded underneath the huge ore hauler, sending it at least thirty meters in the air.

Kell noted with satisfaction that the nearly full load of dilithium was thrown in all directions—many of the crystals flying off into the pit that was just a few meters behind the vehicle.

Then, with a deafening crash, the ore hauler smashed into the ground, twisting itself as it shook the ground under Kell's feet.

"I think we got it," Benitez said. Kell did not have to look to see the smile on his roommate's face.

Then an angry red beam flashed over their heads.

"And it looks like the Orions noticed," Kell said.

Suddenly, other beams started crashing around them. Watching carefully, Kell counted five origin points. He hoped that meant that the Orion he had seen closest to the ore hauler had been incapacitated by its explosion.

With hand motions, he told Benitez to move position. Using cargo containers and support pillars for cover, they made their way closer to the pit.

The typically foolish Orions, however, kept up fire on their previous position. From their new position, they could make out five Orions...no, six. One was lying on the ground, incapacitated.

From the look of the Orion's wound, Kell judged that the incapacitation was permanent.

By now, the fire on their previous position was slowly dissipating and the Orions were elsewhere.

Suddenly, he felt a tremor under his feet. Then he heard the deep rumble of an explosion somewhere underground.

"If that was the warp core..." Benitez said, once again speaking Kell's thoughts out loud.

Then the shaking stopped and Kell said. "I don't think so...we are still here."

When he looked back at the Orions, Kell could see that the shaking had knocked them to the ground. They were slowly picking up their weapons and getting up.

Kell shook his head. They were a pitifully unworthy enemy.

"They outnumber and outgun us, Flash, I say we attack?" Benitez said.

The Klingon nodded. "Let's end this now. The captain may need our help."

Simultaneously, the two officers got up from their crouching positions and raised their weapons. They started running full-out toward the Orions' position, firing as they ran.

Already disoriented from the explosion, the Orions were slow to see them and slower to react. By the time they raised their weapons, Kell had found a target, then another. Benitez found one as well.

Then the two officers let out a battle cry. The remaining two Orions jumped at the sound, but managed to fire in their direction.

Kell saw a blast head over his left shoulder, where Benitez was running. A quick glance told him that his partner was unharmed, and then Kell was looking forward again, firing as he ran. Kell and Benitez fired and struck the last two Orions nearly simultaneously.

The two men came to a stop. Benitez was smiling, and Kell returned the gesture.

"Flash, remind me—"

Before Benitez could finish, Kell did two things simultaneously. He saw movement out of his peripheral vision from somewhere near the control area. Before the movement had completely registered, he dove for the nearest cover, shoving his partner down as he went.

The two men hit the ground with a thud. Benitez, fortunately, had the sense to ask no questions and crawled for better cover, as blasts rang out over their heads.

The fire was heavy, even when they were finally out of the attacker's sight. Kell did not venture a glance from their covered position.

Then the enemy fire was tearing up cargo containers and blasting metal supports all around them. Even if the enemy could not see them, it was only a matter of time until they hit the officers directly or hit something close enough to them to have the same effect.

Kell noted that the enemy was using a different and more powerful weapon than the Orion arms. If he didn't do something soon, he would find out just how much more powerful.

With a wave, he showed Benitez what he wanted to do. The human nodded and the two men made their way closer to the edge of the pit. The cover was not as good, but they were able to make their way to Kell's objective, the twisted hulk that was the ore hauler.

A few moments later both men slipped past a single cargo container and were behind the vehicle. Heavily armored, it provided the best cover in the immediate area. Kell allowed himself a few deep breaths and looked at Benitez.

"At least they are a challenge," Kell said.

"Personally, I liked them better when they were inept," Benitez said, smiling. "What's the plan, Flash?"

Benitez pointed to a support pylon about twenty meters away. "I will run that way to draw their fire. You shoot them all when they reveal themselves to fire."

Benitez nodded seriously. "Okay, but you be careful, Jon," he said.

"You as well, Luis. And do not miss," Kell replied.

He started to turn, already tensing his legs for the leap into action, when the world exploded behind him.

They must have hit the cargo container behind us,

Kell thought as the blast picked him up and tossed him forward.

Benitez, who was closer to the container, overtook him in the air. Even as they flew, Kell saw that Benitez would land close to the edge of the pit, dangerously close.

The Klingon reached out a hand and was able to just feel Benitez's uniform as the human was thrown past him. Then Kell's shoulder struck something solid and he came to a rest on the ground.

Turning his head to look for his partner, he saw Benitez resting precariously near the edge. The human was injured, though Kell could not see how badly.

Kell struggled to clear his vision and tried to determine how badly his own body was damaged.

Then he heard footsteps. They were coming closer.

Reflexively, he reached for his phaser, but the rifle was gone, thrown somewhere by the blast.

When the footsteps seemed almost upon him, he found that his right hand still worked, and reached for his sidearm.

That was gone too.

Chapter Twenty-four

THE EMERGENCY BRIDGE LIGHTS flickered on. The bridge crew seemed unharmed.

"Helm status, Mr. Sulu," Spock said.

"No response, sir," Sulu said.

Spock hit the science-station intercom button and said, "Spock to engineering."

"Scott here," said the chief engineer's voice.

"Mr. Scott, I need emergency power to the helm and functional thrusters immediately," Spock said.

"Is that all?" Mr. Scott said.

"Yes, that will be sufficient for the moment," Spock replied.

"Sir, we just had a hell of a whallop and my equipment must be faulty because it's telling me that we are inside the outer layer of a red giant."

The Vulcan ignored the chief engineer's comment. "Time for repairs?" Spock asked.

"Time for repairs?" Scott said and Spock could clearly hear exasperation in the human's voice. "Pick your system, we're still inventorying damage."

Spock checked the shield level. They were at forty-two percent and falling.

"Mr. Scott, unless we have helm control and thrusters in forty-eight seconds, the shields will fail. Then you will be able to measure our survival time in hundredths of a second."

There was silence on the intercom for a moment. Spock took the time to calculate the actual amount of the *Enterprise*'s hull that would remain intact after complete shield failure. Taking into consideration temperature of the surrounding stellar material and the insulating properties of the hull material, he concluded that the hull would last exactly .0347 seconds.

"Try it now," said Mr. Scott's voice.

"Mr. Sulu, take us out," Spock said.

"Aye," Sulu said, manipulating his controls. There was a slight but noticeable delay and then the ship was under way.

Spock tracked the ship's progress. They had covered most of the distance to open space before the blast.

Turning to the viewscreen, Spock saw the deep red give way to lighter and lighter shades.

Then the vessel was in open space.

Turning back to the computer, he saw that they had escaped by a comfortable margin: just over 18.06 seconds.

He noticed that the entire bridge crew was looking at him, expectantly.

"The ship is safe," he said.

Spock returned to the command chair and notice that the doctor was clutching the back of it tightly.

"Do not be alarmed, Doctor, we escaped with a safety margin of more than eighteen seconds," the Vulcan said.

That must have satisfied McCoy, because the doctor was speechless for a moment.

Then Chief Engineer Scott entered the bridge. Spock had served among humans long enough to read the displeasure on Mr. Scott's face.

"How long before we have warp speed, Mr. Scott?" Spock asked.

"How long?" the human said, with an expression that Spock could not read. "You can have it now and for about two more hours."

"Please explain," the Vulcan said.

"The stellar flare hit us very hard. The dilithium chamber is damaged and the crystals are failing. You have warp speed for two more hours, then nothing short of a starbase repair station will get this ship past sublight."

Without hesitation, Spock turned to Mr. Sulu and said, "Maximum warp to System 7348."

Then Spock took a moment to calculate the time required to reach the system at maximum warp. Then he subtracted the time lost due to loss of speed during the final decay of the dilithium reaction chamber.

He concluded that they would reach the system with several minutes to spare. Turning back to the chief engineer, he said, "Excellent, that will be fine, Mr. Scott."

To the Vulcan's surprise, the human did not seem pleased. Instead, he shook his head and muttered something indistinguishable as he headed for the turbolift.

Kirk saw the warp reactor looming up ahead as he ran. The large vertical cylinder that glowed with blue light was huge, much larger than the ones he had seen on starships. It extended past the hundred-meter height of the ceiling and deep into the floor of the chamber as well.

He realized that it was even bigger even than the ones he had seen that powered some of the larger starbases.

Kirk noted that its power output must be enormous. And in just minutes that power would be directed toward the core of this planet. The results would be catastrophic.

But they wouldn't let that happen.

Scanning the area, he didn't see any Orions, which made sense. They understood the danger better than anyone.

Still, something did not feel right.

He slowed his pace. Chief Brantley did the same beside him, and the others followed suit.

Kirk turned to see that Ensign Jawer had his tricorder out. "There's no one here. It's unprotected," he said.

"That's what worries me," Kirk said.

But the ensign was already stepping around Chief Brantley. "If I can get in there quickly."

"Wait—" Kirk said.

Brantley moved quickly, grabbing Jawer by the shoulder and pulling him back.

"What?" the young ensign said.

Brantley raised his phaser rifle and pointed it at the floor just a few meters in front of their position.

He fired and the beam was immediately absorbed by

a large forcefield that flared brightly. From the flash, Kirk could see that the forcefield extended the thirty-meter width and approximately one-hundred-meter height of the outer entrance of the reactor chamber.

"Oh, sorry, sir," Jawer said.

Kirk pointed to a bank of controls and consoles near the entrance. "Can you shut it off?"

Jawer looked at the controls, then back to the forcefield. Kirk could see an idea form on the ensign's face.

He lifted his phaser and said, "Actually, I think there is an even quicker way, Captain."

Kirk smiled and said, "Be my guest, Ensign."

Jawer stepped to the side of the corridor and motioned everyone to do the same.

Then he raised his weapon and pointed it at the far right side of the forcefield, just past where the field emitters would be.

Though the field emitters themselves were protected by the forcefield, the wall that held them in place was not.

Jawer's beam cut directly into the wall. Kirk could see the flare when the red beam struck metal. The wall was reinforced and could have withstood any standard-issue side arm...

...but not a Starfleet phaser rifle set for a full-power blast.

Using the beam to cut downward, Jawer sliced away at the frame that defined the entrance to the reactor chamber. Large chunks of metal fell away.

Then the right side of the entrance started to fall. The field emitters on the right side of the field were denied power and the entire forcefield shorted out in a brilliant flash that left bright afterimage on Kirk's vision.

Kirk smiled at the ensign. "An impressive display, Mr. Jawer."

"Thank you, sir," he replied.

"Let's move," Kirk said, heading for the reactor at a run.

There were banks of computer terminals and control consoles. Most of them were mysteries to Kirk, but they seemed to make sense to Jawer as he quickly scanned each one.

He settled on one console and said, "This is the master control panel, sir."

The others converged on the station to watch the ensign work. He flipped a switch and one of the monitors came alive with a countdown in English numerals.

They had less than seven minutes to go.

Jawer studied the rest of the controls in front of him for a moment. Then he hit a series of switches and buttons.

"Captain, this one should do it," he said, pointing to a single, green switch.

"Any chance of booby traps?" Kirk asked.

"Unlikely, sir. Warp systems, particularly these large ones, are designed with many redundant safety protocols. The Orions turned them all off, but they likely didn't have time to program anything as elaborate as a booby trap—which the master computer might have rejected anyway."

"Are you sure, Ensign?" Kirk asked.

Jawer didn't flinch. "Yes, sir." Kirk noticed that in this area, the young man had complete confidence.

"Do you give the word, Captain?" Jawer asked him.

"The word is given, Ensign," Kirk said.

Jawer hit the switch.

For a long moment, nothing happened. Then a low hum filled the room.

The warp core pulsed for a moment. Then the blue light that ran its entire length pulsed and faded. Then Kirk saw a change near the ceiling. The warp core was going dark from the top down. The same thing was happening from the floor up.

The blue light of the reactor was shrinking toward its own center.

Then the shadows that replaced the shrinking blue light met and the warp core was dark.

The hum also died, and Kirk knew it was over.

"Excellent work," he said. "Now, let's pick up Anderson and Benitez and get back to the surface."

"These two are alive," someone said. There was clear malice in the voice, and something else, something familiar that he could not place.

Kell struggled to get up. He would face this foe on his feet.

Summoning all of his strength, he managed to pull himself to his knees, before a boot-clad foot struck him, hard, in the ribs and forced him onto his side.

From his new position, he could see Benitez clearly. The human was injured, but moving. Like Kell, he was trying to orient himself and looking around for the enemy.

Darkness threatened to engulf Kell, but he fought it back. He had seen something, something important.

Forcing his eyes open, he saw what it was. Benitez's uniform was drawn up on one side, revealing the phaser 2 that was still there.

The human was shaking his head, no doubt trying to

clear it. Did Benitez know it was there? Would there be time to use it against their enemy?

Then Kell saw that Benitez was reaching for something, for his phaser, but his movements were sluggish.

Then Kell saw two boot-clad feet striding over to Benitez's position.

"Not so fast, Earther," a voice said, and one of the boots lashed out at Benitez.

But the human was very near the edge of the pit.

"No!" Kell called out. Before he realized he was doing it, he was getting quickly to his feet—quickly enough to see another kick to Benitez's side, this one knocking the phaser off him and out of reach. One more kick and the human would go over the side.

Kell took a step toward Benitez, who met his eyes for a moment.

Then a hand grabbed Kell and he was spun around to face his enemy.

For a moment, he thought he must be looking at one of Gorath's warriors, but this Klingon was wearing the uniform of the Klingon Defense Force.

Kell saw that the Klingon was pointing a heavy disruptor straight at his chest. Then Kell realized what had been familiar about the voice he had heard—it had been speaking Klingon. Not the ancient Klingon of Gorath's people, but the current tongue of the Empire.

The Klingon was sneering at him and said. "Don't worry, you will die with your fellow Earther."

Kell's vision was very clear now. He saw that the Klingon pointing a weapon at him was a low-ranking one—someone's personal guard. So was the Klingon standing over Benitez.

Their leader was studying Kell with interest. He wore the uniform of a Klingon high commander and there was something familiar about him.

Then the Klingon guard close to him pushed Kell toward Benitez and the pit.

"Wait," the officer said, approaching Kell. "I know this one."

The guard gave his commander a look of dumb disappointment, but put his hand down.

The officer came closer, studying Kell. Surprise registered on his face.

"betleH 'etlh SoH" Or, in English, "You are the Blade of the Bath'leth."

"I serve the Empire," Kell said in Klingon, giving the response.

"Jon, what—" Then a booted foot struck Benitez, not hard enough to put him over the edge, but enough to silence him. Kell remembered that his roommate spoke Klingon, or at least understood it.

He also remembered that Benitez had learned it to win something called a Galactic Citizenship badge as a young man. Kell shook his head. The humans had courage and could perform great feats, but they were painfully naïve.

"Have you completed your mission? Is Kirk dead?" the officer said. Then Kell remembered where he had seen the Klingon before. It was shortly after his surgery. The high commander had inspected all of the Infiltrators in his group before Kell had been sent on his mission—before he had been sent to the *Enterprise*.

"No," Kell said, but his mind was already filling with questions. "The Orions?" he asked.

"They are dead," the officer said. "They were useful to us, but not anymore."

"Useful?" Kell asked.

"They are *targs,* they did some tasks for us, built and ran this complex," the officer said.

"But those of our blood on the surface?" Kell said.

"Yes, they fought well and killed all of the Orion *targs* on the surface," the officer said, smiling.

Kell found his blood boiling as his understanding grew. "This complex would have destroyed them all— and they are of our blood. They carry the blood of our honored ancestors."

The Klingon officer's eyes were cold. "They are an unfortunate loss, but one that we have to bear."

Kell could not believe the officer's words.

"This is war!" the Klingon high commander shouted. Then he smiled and said, "If you want to eat pipius claw you have to break a few pipiuses."

Then the officer gave Benitez's guard a signal, and the guard gave Benitez a single hard push with one boot.

"No!" Kell called out, but before the word was out of his mouth, his partner and friend had disappeared into the pit.

The officer looked at him with disdain. "You value those cowardly Earthers? They have contaminated you. It was a concern for the Infiltrator project. Fortunately, some of you remember their duty."

The officer headed for the transporter pad, motioning for his two guards to follow. The officer stepped onto the pad and turned to face him.

"Now you can die with your precious Earthers." He checked his chronometer and said, "Very soon."

Then a Klingon transporter beam took him.

Kell could not believe what he had just witnessed.

This was not the Empire he served. That Empire had been forged when Kahless the Unforgettable forged the first *bat'leth*. Its path had been set when Kahless used the blade to slay the tyrant Molor. And its destiny sealed with the blood of every Klingon who died with honor and met Kahless on the other side of the River of Blood, in *Sto-Vo-Kor*.

"Jon," a thin voice said, breaking the terrible silence around him.

"Jon," it repeated.

Before his mind registered the meaning of the sound, he was running to the edge of the pit.

Benitez was there, clutching metal tubing and hanging over the abyss. Automatically, Kell climbed down the necessary steps and lowered his hand to Benitez.

Then he stopped himself.

"Jon," Benitez said, straining.

Kell thought of the Klingon high commander, who would sacrifice a planet full of Klingons to win a war that should never be fought.

"I cannot betray my Empire, my people, my blood," he said to Benitez, pulling his hand back.

An understanding that Benitez had obviously been fighting crossed his face. "You're a Klingon."

"Yes," Kell replied, speaking the truth to his partner and friend for the first time since they met.

Benitez's hands began to slip and he struggled to adjust his grip.

"Help me. This isn't you, I know you. I know you, Jon. Help me and we can go to the captain. He'll do something…he'll help you. Help me, Jon. Don't do this. This isn't you."

Tears were streaming openly on the human's face now. Jon understood why, though his own Klingon eyes had no tear ducts.

It took all of Kell's will to keep from reaching his hand down to his friend. But once he did that, he was exposed, and so were the dozens, perhaps hundreds of Infiltrators who were now throughout the Federation.

The Empire might destroy itself in its quest to destroy the Federation, but he would not aid that destruction.

He had lost so much of his honor, he would not forget his duty to his people.

"I'm sorry, Luis. This *is* who I am," he said finally.

"I can't hold on!" Benitez said.

"I am sorry."

Then he saw that Benitez finally understood. The human had seen into Kell's heart and saw that he would find no help there.

The next look shamed Kell, because it was angry, defiant, and carried a terrible judgment.

Still, Kell did not look away. He held Benitez's eyes, the eyes of the only friend he now had, human or Klingon.

He saw his own shame, his treachery, his dishonor and the final judgment on his honor.

Benitez was slipping again, but he found strength in his defiance.

"It won't work, you Klingon bastard. He'll stop you. The captain will stop you," Benitez said. "You Klingons sell out your own kind. You won't win," the human spat. Kell could see that the skin on his partner's right forearm was torn. That hand was weakest and let go of the pipe first.

The left hand soon followed, and Benitez fell, screaming.

The screams sounded for what seemed like a long time. And then, even when they faded, Kell could still see Benitez falling.

Then his friend finally disappeared into the darkness of the abyss.

Chapter Twenty-five

KELL WAS SITTING next to the pit when he heard movement behind him. There were voices, they were speaking to him, but he could not hear them over the roar of his blood.

There was a hand on his face. It was gentle, smooth.

"He looks all right, Captain," a voice said. He recognized it. Parrish.

Her face was in front of his. Then he was standing up, though it must have been through her action, because he was not aware of any motion in his own body.

Then the captain was in front of him, his face full of concern.

"The planet is safe," Kirk said. Then the captain looked around, taking in the scene.

"You destroyed the crystals?" Kirk asked, the voice bringing him back, quieting the roar in his blood by a small measure.

Then he remembered. He had a duty. He had to report to this man who had saved his life.

"Yes, most of them," he said.

"Ensign Benitez?" Kirk asked him.

"Dead," Kell said, gesturing to the pit.

Parrish made a sound; then a hand was on his shoulder. It was hers; he recognized the touch.

"I'm sorry," the captain said.

Kell could see that the others were looking at him with feeling. There was a human word for it...sympathy.

It shamed him. He deserved nothing, having cast the last shred of his honor into the pit with Benitez.

Still his mind took inventory. Brantley was alive. And Clark. And Jawer.

They had all survived except for Sobel and Benitez.

Kirk's communicator chirped.

"Kirk here," he said.

"*Enterprise* here, Captain," the Vulcan's voice said.

"Once again, Mr. Spock, your timing is impeccable," Kirk said.

"I do not understand," the Vulcan said.

"I will explain in person, Spock. Six to beam up."

A moment later the roar in his blood, his mind, and his ears was replaced by a different roar as the transporter beam took him.

Lieutenant West reached the admiral's office just behind Ensign Hatcher, who was carrying a tray that contained his lunch and the admiral's.

Normally, he would have closed the gap between them and said hello out of politeness if nothing else.

But the incident outside of her quarters had been only

last night. Though West was still not sure exactly what had happened, he was sure that Hatcher was not interested in him. In fact, she seemed to actively dislike him.

That was partially his fault. He had tried to shift their relationship to a personal level. Of course, he had not known at the time that for her the level included loathing.

So West decided that he would keep their interaction entirely professional. If nothing else, it would allow him to avoid compounding his embarrassment.

Walking a few meters behind her, he noted that her walk was still different. Whatever the injury was, it must have been still bothering her.

She stepped into the admiral's office. It was just a few meters more until she reached the admiral, who was standing in front of his desk, waiting for West.

Then West noted that there was something else different about her: her legs, at least the portion that was not concealed by the duty skirt and high boots. They were swollen. No, not swollen, thicker.

Suddenly, a terrible realization filled him. *That is not Yeoman Hatcher.*

As that thought rose up in his mind, he saw her remove one hand from the tray and use it to throw off the cover.

By the time he saw that she was reaching inside, he was already running and shouting "Admiral!" at the top of his voice.

He raced for her and for the admiral. As he stepped just behind her, he used his left hand to grab her by the shoulder and pull, spinning her off balance.

Thinking of the admiral, West leapt in front of her. He was in front of the admiral now and turning. Facing the intruder, he saw a brief flash of metal, then felt only pressure as the blade penetrated his stomach.

Acting reflexively, he reached out and pushed with both hands. He caught her off balance and she stumbled backward.

Turning to look over his right shoulder, he saw the admiral raising a phaser that had somehow appeared in his hand.

The admiral fired once and the beam sent the intruder stumbling back to the floor.

Incredibly, she got up immediately and ran for the door. In the outer office, she lunged for the security guard and a moment later had his phaser in her hand. She adjusted it and fired it point-blank at the stunned guard, who disappeared in a flash of light.

Then she pointed the weapon directly into the office, straight at Admiral Justman, and fired. It hit the emergency forcefield that now covered the admiral's door with great force, causing it to spark and ripple with energy, but the field held.

She tried again but the forcefield was too strong.

Then she turned her head sharply to look at motion behind her.

Turning back to face Justman and West, she gave them a disgusted look and pointed the phaser at her own chest.

A moment later, she disappeared in a great flash of red light.

"Patrick," someone said to him.

Turning his head, he saw that the admiral was looking at him with concern. Then he felt himself sinking. He would have fallen if not for the admiral's hands on him.

Admiral Justman lowered him gently to the floor.

Then the admiral was shouting. "I need an emergency beam-out! Straight to medical...then get the damn forcefield off!"

A moment later, West felt the room swirl around him.

"Stay with me, son," the admiral said.

The room held its shape again.

"You are going to be fine. That's an order," the admiral said, his hands supporting West's head.

"Yes, sir," West said.

Then he felt a transporter beam take him. Looking up, he could see that it was taking the admiral as well.

About the Author

Kevin Ryan is the author of two novels and the co-author of two more. He has written a bunch of comic books and has also written for television. He lives in New York with his wife and four children. He can be reached at Kryan1964@aol.com.

Look for STAR TREK fiction from Pocket Books

Star Trek®

Star Trek®: Day of Honor

#1 • *Ancient Blood* • Diane Carey
#2 • *Armageddon Sky* • L.A. Graf
#3 • *Her Klingon Soul* • Michael Jan Friedman
#4 • *Treaty's Law* • Dean Wesley Smith & Kristine Kathryn Rusch
The Television Episode • Michael Jan Friedman
Day of Honor Omnibus • various

Star Trek®: The Captain's Table

#1 • *War Dragons* • L.A. Graf
#2 • *Dujonian's Hoard* • Michael Jan Friedman
#3 • *The Mist* • Dean Wesley Smith & Kristine Kathryn Rusch
#4 • *Fire Ship* • Diane Carey
#5 • *Once Burned* • Peter David
#6 • *Where Sea Meets Sky* • Jerry Oltion
The Captain's Table Omnibus • various

Star Trek®: The Dominion War

#1 • *Behind Enemy Lines* • John Vornholt
#2 • *Call to Arms...* • Diane Carey
#3 • *Tunnel Through the Stars* • John Vornholt
#4 • *...Sacrifice of Angels* • Diane Carey

Star Trek®: Section 31™

Rogue • Andy Mangels & Michael A. Martin
Shadow • Dean Wesley Smith & Kristine Kathryn Rusch
Cloak • S.D. Perry
Abyss • David Weddle & Jeffrey Lang

Star Trek®: Gateways

#1 • *One Small Step* • Susan Wright
#2 • *Chainmail* • Diane Carey
#3 • *Doors Into Chaos* • Robert Greenberger
#4 • *Demons of Air and Darkness* • Keith R.A. DeCandido
#5 • *No Man's Land* • Christie Golden
#6 • *Cold Wars* • Peter David
#7 • *What Lay Beyond* • various
Epilogue: Here There Be Monsters • Keith R.A. DeCandido

Star Trek®: The Badlands

#1 • Susan Wright
#2 • Susan Wright

Star Trek®: Dark Passions

#1 • Susan Wright
#2 • Susan Wright

Star Trek® Omnibus Editions

Invasion! Omnibus • various
Day of Honor Omnibus • various
The Captain's Table Omnibus • various
Star Trek: Odyssey • William Shatner with Judith and Garfield Reeves-Stevens
Millennium Omnibus • Judith and Garfield Reeves-Stevens
Starfleet: Year One • Michael Jan Friedman

Other Star Trek® Fiction

Legends of the Ferengi • Ira Steven Behr & Robert Hewitt Wolfe
Strange New Worlds, vol. I, II, III, IV, and V • Dean Wesley Smith, ed.
Adventures in Time and Space • Mary P. Taylor, ed.
Captain Proton: Defender of the Earth • D.W. "Prof" Smith
New Worlds, New Civilizations • Michael Jan Friedman
The Lives of Dax • Marco Palmieri, ed.
The Klingon Hamlet • Wil'yam Shex'pir
Enterprise Logs • Carol Greenburg, ed.
Amazing Stories Anthology • various